THE
SAGA
OF
MARY JO

A Political Virgin
With Stars in Her Eyes
And Kool-Aid on Her Lips

a novel by

Dr. Kelly Swifte

The Saga of Mary Jo, A Political Virgin With Stars In Her Eyes And Kool-aid On Her Lips, is a work of political satire. The story is fictional and does not represent any actual person or event.

Dr. Kelly Swifte
www.politicalvirgin.com
Website design by DogOnCrack

ISBN-978-0-615-36506-0

For all the Mary Jos . . .
past, present and future.

And for my fellow Bunkerites,
you know who you are!

THE
SAGA
OF
MARY JO

**A Political Virgin
With Stars in Her Eyes
And Kool-Aid on Her Lips**

Prologue
First Contact

Mary Jo had never been to a political rally before. Her friend was meeting her right up by the stage, but she was running late and the rally was so crowded she didn't think she'd ever find Jane. It was exciting, but the yelling and chanting of "Obantam, Obantam" made her uneasy. Many looked like they were in a trance. She wanted to get away, but more people had moved in behind her. Some glared at her, as if she was doing something wrong by not joining in with their chanting. She looked around and saw others who weren't chanting. They looked as uncomfortable as she supposed she must.

"The only way to get through this," thought Mary Jo, "is to join them." She began yelling and high-fiving and fist bumping everyone she saw, joining in the chant, but all the while moving closer to the stage where she could just make out Jane's sign. After much deliberation, Jane had painted a huge heart with 'Jane + Banty' boldly painted in the center.

"Jane," yelled Mary Jo, "JANE!"

"Jane," moaned the crowd. "JANE!" The moan grew louder. "JANE HONDA is here! This is her daughter! Let her through!" The crowd went wild and parted like the Red Sea. Mary Jo ran through the aisle and right into Jane's arms. The glorious being on the stage smiled dazzlingly and nodded approvingly. Mary Jo suddenly felt wonderful and was so glad she'd come to the rally.

"Here," said Jane, holding a cup brimming with a bright blue liquid to Mary Jo's lips. "You drink this. I've had enough." Jane laughed with blue-stained lips as Mary Jo sniffed the liquid. "It's totally safe, silly! It's kool-aid!"

"It's not like it's alcohol or anything dangerous," thought Mary Jo as she drank. Up on stage, the magnetic, hypnotic young man smiled and applauded her and promised that he'd be her President. Mary Jo drank even deeper and suddenly swooned. And when she awoke . . . there were stars in her eyes and kool-aid on her lips.

Chapter 1
Roofied!

Mary Jo's eyelashes fluttered weakly. She felt a strong hand grasping hers and someone was gently blotting her hot forehead with a damp cloth. "Where am I?" she wondered. The heat and the noise of the crowd was gone. The slight sway and a steady thrumming rhythm made her suspect she was in a moving vehicle. "But it's a bed," she exclaimed as she bolted upright and shook off the hand that clasped hers.

"There, there," said a deep mellifluous voice. "Everything's fine. We thought we'd lost you."

"W-w-w-where am I?" stammered Mary Jo. "Aren't you . . ."

"Yes," soothed the voice. "Call me Barty. No one's called me that since my dear departed momma and grandmomma. It'll be our little pet name, kind of a code. Sorry, but I didn't catch your name when I whisked you away from that little blonde freak, Jane."

"Jane's my friend," said Mary Jo, struggling to rise. "Where is she? She wouldn't go off and leave me like this. I don't even know you. I don't know where we are, and I know you're married! Stop this vehicle, I want to get out!"

"There, there, now, I've remembered. Jane called you Mary Jo. That's a lovely name. Just lie back. Close your eyes and rest. Just listen to my voice. Isn't it soothing? Isn't it reasonable? Don't you want to do what my voice tells you? Of course you do! You just want to relax and let old Uncle Barty get a little bit better acquainted with you. Isn't this nice?! I love blonde hair and yours is so pretty and soft. So are you a natural blonde? I mean to say, does the collar match the cuff?"

"Nooooo," moaned Mary Jo.

"You know, I think you might need a refreshing drink of my special, super tasty drink. It's very special, triple delicious and no alcohol in it at all. I saw you enjoying some with Jane, your lips are still stained all blue. Yes, I definitely think you need hydration, and there's nothing better for that than this." Barty held a cup to Mary Jo's lips and she drank it down.

"Now where were we? Oh yes, I was about to get to know you better, wasn't I, Mary Jo?"

But Mary Jo couldn't answer. She was in a deep hypnotic trance.

Chapter 2
Recruited

"**O**kay, Mary Jo, let's get down to business," said Barty. He kicked off his shoes, stripped off his jacket and tie. He leaned back in a recliner and lit a cigarette. He took a deep drag and blew smoke in Mary Jo's face. She wrinkled her nose reflexively, but remained in a trance.

"You've been recruited, Mary Jo. I need an army of mindless, suggestible and compliant worker bees. You'll do just fine. I have a special task for you, Mary Jo. You're not stupid, just ignorant, and now we can keep it that way. I want you to take this special phone. Someone will call daily with your marching orders and talking points. I want you to read Rules for Radicals and learn how to attack anyone who says a bad word about me. That will make them back down. I want you to wait a few months after I become President, then roam the CoxNews blogs and spew hatred and nonsense and lies all over that network. I'm going to destroy Cox and you'll be one of my tools."

"But I like Cox," muttered Mary Jo. "Cox & Hens on weekends, with Alice . . ."

"Forget that," demanded Barty. "You HATE Cox! Alice is NOT your friend! Your job is to be a total twit who'll annoy conservatives so much they'll be distracted from what I'm doing. What's that, Twit? You want to know what I'm doing? I'm taking over the country! I'm going to grow government so big three out of every five Americans will be government employees! I'm forming a giant global government and Europe and Russia and the Middle East and Africa and all the rest love me so much, they'll make me King! You're a fool, Mary Jo, you don't even know you're being used by the future King of the World!"

"Now listen up. Your new heroes are mainstream media. They're all loyal to me, me, me and will slant you in the right direction. You know, Olberwoman, Maddcow, that Morning Java fool, Mathscrews, the Puffington Postal . . . you get the idea. Listen to them, take their talking points and use them against conservatives. And forget any real history you ever knew or thought you knew. We'll give you a whole new revised history of the United States to quote," said Barty, as he lit another cigarette from the stub of the first.

Chapter 3
Domestic Bliss?

"**O**h, Chad," sighed Mary Jo, " I don't know what's wrong with me. I just don't feel well."

"Well," said Chad, "maybe you should consider a few lifestyle changes."

"Chad! I've been waiting and waiting and thought you'd never pop the question! Of course I'll marry you!"

"Actually, Mary Jo, that wasn't a proposal. You've changed over the past few months and I'm not sure we have enough in common anymore to make this permanent," said Chad.

"Chad, we have so much in common! We both HATE CoxNews and we LOVE Bar – er, Banty. You voted for him, you agreed with all that spending and borrowing just like I did!"

"I should have told you this before, Mary Jo, but you've been acting so weird about Cox lately. I've been watching them, and I think they're the only network getting the facts out and asking the hard questions. You should try it. I think if you'd just give Heck a chance . . ."

Mary Jo's shriek cut him off. "HECK!!! Oh my God, you've been watching HECK!!! I don't know you at all, Chad Sixpack. You're not the man I thought you were! Sneaking around behind my back and watching Cox, how could you?" screamed Mary Jo.

"Shhh . . . we don't need the cops here," warned Chad. "Keep it down. I was just fooling around! Can't you take a joke anymore?" He quickly tried to pacify Mary Jo.

"Ha," said Mary Jo weakly. "I guess I'm just a little stressed. You know, with my father being a Republican, and all the blogging I do with those crazy conservatives . . . I think I'll pour myself a nice glass of kool-aid, put my feet up and rest a bit. Care to join me? I've got plenty of kool-aid."

"Uh . . . I know you've got plenty, Mary Jo, but no thanks. That's really one of the lifestyle changes I was talking about. Maybe you should slow down on drinking that stuff. Try something more substantial – like some red meat for a change. How about I take you out for a nice, juicy, rare steak tonight?" asked Chad.

"Eeuuwww!" Mary Jo wrinkled her nose. "That sounds awful."

"But you used to love . . ."

"Tell you what, you can take me out to our favorite Mexican restaurant. I can have nachos and Flan and you can have steak fajitas! How's that for a compromise? But I have to get to bed early. I need to be rested up for Cox & Hens early tomorrow. I plan on doing some serious conservative butt-kicking. They're all worried about what I'll write about them in my paper. I've got them believing I'm writing a paper about the New Republicans!"

"Whatever," said Chad. "Just leave the kool-aid at home this time, okay? They told you the last three times we were there that they can't make a Margarita with it. Where do you get that stuff anyway, and why does it come by courier every Thursday morning?"

"I told you before, Chad. My Uncle sends it to me. He loves me so much he wants to make sure I have a constant supply of my favorite drink," parroted Mary Jo woodenly.

Chapter 4
Discovery

"Chad, old pal, old friend, I'm afraid I've got some bad news for you," said the voice on the phone.

"Give it to me straight, Buzz, I can take it," Chad told his old college roomie. "I had a feeling something was wrong and I knew you'd get to the bottom of it. I never thought I'd be calling a CSI guy to snoop on my girlfriend though!

"Don't sweat it," said Buzz. "You did the right thing. You could be in some serious danger though. Why don't you pack a bag and come stay with me for awhile?"

"You're kidding, right? Mary Jo wouldn't hurt me, it's just not in her," protested Chad. "Last week she got so out of control with that waiter, threatening to have him fired and screaming that it was all Bush's fault that she couldn't get a kool-aid Margarita, that I was worried she was going to punch him out. I just don't think she'd ever hurt *me* though. So what's in that kool-aid, anyway?"

"It's the blue pill, pal," whispered Buzz. "You didn't drink any of that stuff, did you?"

"Well, just a little. And just at first, when I was trying to get close to her . . . you know. But it was too sweet and kind of moldy tasting. And my teeth and lips turned blue. I told her I had blood sugar issues, so I couldn't drink it anymore. She still tries to get me to drink it, but I won't," said Chad. "What's the story on this blue pill?"

"She's in the Beltway, and you're really lucky you're not there with her! You had a narrow escape, old pal. You'd better be thanking God you didn't drink more of that stuff! See what I mean about coming to stay with me?" asked Buzz.

"Buzz, this is *Mary Jo*, I'm sure I'm safe. But what can I do for her? How can I help her? I can't just go off and leave her like this. What's this Beltway thing? You don't mean those old DC brain-washing rumors, do you?"

"You didn't think those were just idle rumors, did you? Ha, that's a good one! No, she's in the Beltway, about as far away from reality as you can get. The only thing you can do to get her out of it is to give her the red pill. You better think long and hard about that – it's not easy to do. It's dangerous, you have to travel far and she'll fight you every step of the way," explained Buzz. "Is she worth it?"

"I don't know anymore," Chad admitted, "but she's still a human being. And what kind of a person would I be if I didn't try to help her? I have to admit that travel sounds good. I wouldn't mind taking a break from Mary Jo!"

"Sorry, pal, but she's got to go with you. It's a long trip and like I said, she'll fight you every step of the way. Are you sure you're up for it?" Buzz asked.

"I guess I don't have much choice," Chad replied. "Where do I have to go? I guess no place in the world is farther away than a day's travel by airplane."

"Yeah, too bad you can't take a plane," said Buzz. "Or any public transportation, for that matter. With that blue pill in her cells, she'll light up security like you wouldn't believe. Then they just keep tracking her. As soon as they see where she's headed, they'll stop you, throw you in prison and return her to her assigned duties."

"Wow," said Chad, "this is some scary stuff." He took a deep breath. "Okay, I'll try it. Where do we have to go to get the red pill?"

"You go north, Chad, north," said his friend.

"Canada?" asked Chad.

"Nope. North of Canada.

"Alaska? You can't mean . . ."

"Yep, old pal, Rogue Peyton has the red pills. And you have to get there before she starts campaigning in the Lower 48. She'll be in the spotlight then and anyone who contacts her will be scrutinized by the powers that be."

Chapter 5
Surprise

"Mary Jo, I have a surprise for you," said Chad.

"Hummmmmm . . . not now, I'm busy," muttered Mary Jo as she sat hunched over the computer keyboard.

"C'mon, Mary Jo, you can take a break and listen to my surprise. I planned it especially for you. Please? For me?"

"I told you, I'm busy, you moron! Now I forgot what I wanted to say to this megawitch on Alice's blog. Oh, I'm so mad at you! Just when I was going to let her have it with both barrels! Now STOP BOTHERING ME!" she screamed.

"Mary Jo, are you all right? This isn't like you at all. You're acting weird!

"Oh, Chad. I'm so sorry. I am fine. Nothing is wrong," Mary Jo said in a monotone as she turned away from the computer. "Don't worry about it. I'm the same person I always was."

"No, you're a different person. Sometimes I hardly know you. We used to have fun. You used to love surprises. Now I just bother you."

"I am fine. Nothing is wrong," Mary Jo repeated in the same monotone. "What was your surprise?"

"I thought we'd take a little trip. You love Canada and it's beautiful up there. You want to know more about their healthcare, we could check it out while we enjoy a vacation too."

"Canada. I don't know. Can I take a trip right now?" Mary Jo seemed to direct her question to the ceiling light fixture. "Canada. I could video people there who love their healthcare and post it on Alice's peagreenroom blog to prove my point. Sure, why not? As long as I can continue blogging from there. I'll need a laptop and extra kool-aid." Mary Jo again spoke to the fixture, then turned to Chad. "When did you want to go, Chad? We'll need to make reservations."

"No reservations necessary, we're taking a road trip! Look, it's only a half hour to the border from Troy, we can leave early next morning. Let's try to get up into the *real* Canada, not so close to the U.S. Border. I bet you'll get the truth about their healthcare system that way. You could be an on-the-road correspondent! That would show those conservative bloggers. We could stay at B&Bs and explore Canada when you're not working on your reporting or blogging. It'll be way better than a quick fly-in," Chad assured her.

"That would show them all, wouldn't it," mused Mary Jo. "Okay, Chad, let's do it! I must admit, I didn't think you were so concerned or would be so supportive of my work. It's crucial to get people to stop fighting this healthcare thing. You were right, this is a great surprise!"

"I'm just trying to help you, Mary Jo, I'm just trying to help you. Now where are we going to get you a laptop?"

"Oh, don't worry about that. Tomorrow's Thursday. I'm sure Uncle would love to give me one." Mary Jo looked at the light fixture again. "If he can get the laptop to me with extra kool-aid in tomorrow's delivery, we can leave right after. I'm getting excited about this trip. What a good idea this was, Chad!"

"We can only hope, Mary Jo, we can only hope," said Chad as he went off to pack.

Chapter 6
Ready, Set . . .

"Chad," laughed Mary Jo, looking at the stack of luggage. "I thought you said we'd be gone for about ten days. This looks like enough stuff for a month, at least!"

"Well, I figured I'd have some time to kill. I know you'll be busy with blogging and getting information from real Canadians about how much they love their nationalized healthcare. I don't want to get in your way or interfere with your work, so I brought some extra stuff. You know, sports stuff," explained Chad.

"Sure. Good idea. Maybe you can rent a bike."

"That's what I thought! I packed my helmet, shoes and pads, . . ."

"That's great," Mary Jo interrupted him. "Sounds good. Where the heck is that courier? I could sure use a kool-aid waker-upper right now. You shouldn't have let me drink so much of it last night. My supply is entirely gone!" Mary Jo nervously rubbed her damp palms together.

"Well, Mary Jo, you wanted to party. As I recall, you finished off the last of the kool-aid just an hour ago, right before your shower. You haven't slept at all, have you?" asked Chad.

"I just wanted to make last night special for you. Was it, Chad? Was it really, *really* special?"

"Yes, it was really, *really* special," replied Chad, repressing a shudder as he recalled how Mary Jo's voracious blue lips had fed off his body last night. "You know, it might be kind of special another way, too . . ."

"You know I only like it one way, Chad," Mary Jo said coldly. "I don't think we need to have this discussion again, especially when we're about to leave for a fabulous trip. Now stop your pouting and let's not talk about this again." Mary Jo opened the front door and looked down the street. "Where the heck is that courier?"

"*Relax*, Mary Jo. Doesn't he always deliver at 8:00 sharp? Well, you've got fifteen minutes to wait. I'll go get the thermoses ready. Black coffee for me, half and half for you. Half coffee and half kool-aid, that is. I'll just put the coffee in now, and as soon as the kool-aid gets here, we'll top off your thermos and hit the road." Chad disappeared into the kitchen while Mary Jo continued to scan the empty street.

Chad shut the kitchen door and pulled a cigar case from its hiding spot in a cupboard. He opened it to reveal a dozen tiny ampules filled with a white powder. He unfolded a paper and reread the instructions that Buzz had provided.

"Am I really going to do this?" Chad wondered as he looked at the powder. "This is drugging and kidnapping and transporting someone over an international border. "*Can* I do this? I was a Boy Scout, never been in trouble of any kind, never even jaywalked. And here I am, preparing to engage in big time crimes. Do I even have a choice? Not really. I guess these are the times that try men's souls," Chad thought, remembering his history lessons.

"Country first," he whispered as he broke the tip off an ampule and poured the contents into Mary Jo's thermos.

Chapter 7
On The Road

Chad kept his eyes on the road and continued driving. Mary Jo still slept deeply, securely buckled into the passenger seat.

"Eight hours," he thought, "she'll wake up soon and want her kool-aid fix. I'm an hour behind schedule. I've got to get there before she wakes up." Chad drove faster as he reviewed his instructions from Buzz.

"You can't just take her off the kool-aid," Buzz had said. "Won't work, no way, no how. You try to make her go cold turkey and she'll go ballistic. I'm serious about this, Chad. She'll rip your head off. Are you listening to me? I mean *really* listening? You can't afford to be casual about this. If she doesn't get that stuff regularly, she'll turn into a raving lunatic, try to kill everyone nearby and then slip into a coma and die."

Chad glanced over at Mary Jo. Her blue lips were sucking furiously at her thumb. "Barty," she moaned, "Barty . . ." She seemed to be waking up.

Chad knew he wouldn't make it to the rendezvous before time ran out. Suddenly his cell phone rang. No, it was his new, prepaid, untraceable cell phone!

Chad fumbled for the phone. "Yes, YES . . . don't hang up! I'm here," he answered, expecting to hear Buzz's voice.

"I know who you are. No names. Don't say a word," said an unfamiliar voice. "We're here to help. You're off schedule, so we're picking you up. Flash your headlights if you understand." Chad complied with the request.

"Fine. Reduce speed to 35mph. Drive straight ahead. Do not alter your speed or trajectory. Do not worry, I repeat, DO NOT WORRY about anything in your path. We are picking you up in exactly 45 seconds," said the voice.

Chad followed instructions and waited to see what would happen. He didn't have to wait long. Directly in front of him loomed a huge Red Mutt beer truck! Chad started to automatically slow down, then recalled his instructions. The back of the trailer opened and a ramp emerged. As Chad held his speed steady, the trailer slowed and his vehicle was swallowed up and jerked to a stop inside by a safety net. Chad killed the engine.

"Where . . ." Mary Jo's eyes suddenly opened. "What's . . ." she began as someone injected her with a bright blue fluid. Her head dropped onto her chest and she began to snore softly.

"What was that?" Chad demanded. "Who are you?"

"Relax, Chad," said the somehow familiar figure. "We're here to help. She'll sleep again, with that dose of concentrated kool-aid and the Mickey Finn. Seems cruel, but it's the best way."

"Thanks," said Chad. "I really appreciate this, and I know Mary Jo does too. I mean, she would if she was herself. Do I know you? You look so familiar."

"You may have seen me on TV. I asked Obantam a question once and my whole life blew up. So now I help where I can. Anything for the cause!" said the man.

"Moe?" gasped Chad, "Moe the Plumber?! "You're kidding me!

Chapter 8
Truckin'

"This is too much," thought Chad. "Just too much for my brain to handle."

Moe must have been reading his mind because he quickly popped open a beer and handed it to Chad. "Drink up, buddy. You need to hydrate," he said.

Chad gulped the beer thankfully. "Funny," he said, "Mary Jo always tells me I need to hydrate. But she wants me to drink the kool-aid."

"Yeah," said Moe, "she's got a bad case of it. I don't believe I've ever seen lips that blue. I just hope and pray we're in time."

"What's the plan? Do you drop us at the B&B?" asked Chad. "We were supposed to meet our connection there. We need to ditch the car, our phones and Mary Jo's laptop. They can track us if we don't!"

"Plans change," said Moe. "Don't worry, we've got you covered. The inside of this trailer is totally impenetrable by any surveillance device known to man. All that shows up on any tracking device is a full load of beer. We are cloaked and stoked, buddy."

"But we can't . . ."

"But you can," Moe said. "Kick back, relax, get a little sleep. There's beer and more beer, food in that cooler and your girlfriend's out for awhile. Take a load off. We might be able to get you all the way to the Alaska border. Worst case scenario, we'll have to drop you with new wheels and identification . . ."

Suddenly a speaker above their heads crackled to life.

"Moe . . . I'll have to stop. There's a barricade up ahead." The speaker went silent.

Moe fiddled with a closed circuit system and a screen showed the road ahead. "WALNUT! Those dirty . . .!" And he grabbed his gun and racked a shell into the chamber.

"Moe, it's okay. Not to worry. I'll take care of it. Everything's under control. Oh my God, they've seen me. They're genuflecting! They love me! We'll have no problems at all!" the voice from the speaker declared.

Moe laughed and put away the gun. "I forgot who we're traveling with," he said. "The only reason WALNUT will stop us is to get an autograph."

"Someone famous, Moe? Driving a beer truck?" asked Chad as the truck stopped.

"Yeah, you'd think those WALNUT fools would wonder what a famous person is doing driving a beer truck in the wilds of Canada. But if they were that bright they might ask themselves why Obantam wanted them manning a barricade in the wilds of Canada! But they just pack up their signs and travel where they're told to and protest what they're told to, and don't ask questions because they're told not to. The bigwigs at WALNUT live large and the little guys get peanuts and kool-aid." Moe stood up and stretched as the truck slowed to s stop. In five minutes they were back on the road.

"So who's driving, Moe?" asked Chad.

"You'll see," chuckled Moe, "you'll see."

Chad leaned back and drank his beer.

"Ninety-nine bottles of beer on the wall . . ." Moe began.

"Ninety-nine bottles of beer . . ." Chad joined in.

Chapter 9
Masquerade

Chad woke when the truck left smooth pavement and bounced over a washboard road. Moe was snoring in the recliner, clutching his Bible with one hand and caressing his gun with the other. Chad looked over at Mary Jo and saw that she was tucked in and sleeping peacefully. She was now contentedly sucking on a baby bottle filled with bright blue liquid.

"I thought it would be easier than an IV," said Moe softly. "I know it doesn't seem right, but look at her. She's happy. When was the last time she was happy?" he asked.

Chad shrugged. "She's happy when she's being mean and vicious on the blogs."

"C'mon, Chad, you know that's the blue pill talking. She'll snap out of it once you get her that red pill," said Moe.

"Moe," came the voice from the speaker. "We've got a problem. This one I can't fix. Seems someone escaped from the fat farm. We'll have to get them different transportation pronto."

The truck came to a stop and in a moment the back of the trailer was opened and the light shone on a portly figure.

"Posie O'Dingbat!" Chad exclaimed, rubbing his eyes. "No way!"

"You got that right, buddy," laughed Moe as he helped Lady Lynx Grove deRougeshield out of the Posie O'Dingbat fat suit while humming the 'Mission: Impossible' theme.

"Got to ditch the truck, Moe," said Lady Lynx. "Posie left the fat farm early and she's all over TV, talking about how they tried to starve her. Can't take a chance of one of those thousands of WALNUT nuts seeing it and reporting Posie driving a beer truck in Canada!"

"Lady Lynx," said Chad, "I wondered what happened to you. After the election you seemed to disappear."

"Ah, but I disappeared with a purpose," said the Lady. "There were plans to be made, plots to be thickened, best to fly under the radar at this point. I'll be speaking out again very soon, when Rogue is free of prior obligations. Oops! Did I say Rogue? Forget you heard that for now, okay?"

"I didn't hear a thing," said Chad, "but tell her I'm very glad."

"You should be able to tell her yourself," said Lady Lynx. "That is, if everything goes right. No reason to think it won't, right, Moe?"

"Righty-tighty, Lady Lynx," agreed Moe. "Here's your new wheels, Chad, and let me just say that it's been a real thrill to meet someone with the last name of Sixpack!" Moe handed him a set of keys and then buckled May Jo into the passenger seat of the 1970 Cougar.

"Barty," moaned Mary Jo, sucking on the empty bottle "Barty . . .?"

"Better get her a refill before you take off," Moe suggested. "There's a cooler in the backseat. It's a good thing you're doing, Chad. I know she's been a pain in the butt liberal moderate progressive rash evil lizard specimen, but she's *your* pain in the butt liberal moderate progressive rash evil lizard specimen!" Moe elbowed Chad in the ribs. "Ha, ha, just kidding, buddy!"

"Thank you," said Chad. "Thank you both so much! I don't know how I can ever repay you."

"No need," said Lady Lynx, "Just keep up the fight. You still have a long way to go, better get moving," she said as she kissed him on the cheek and handed him a map.

Chapter 10
Riding Shotgun

Chad drove on into the dark woods. He thought about all that had happened in the past day. It didn't seem possible that he'd left his old life, left his country and was fleeing through the wilds of Canada with Mary Jo. All he'd ever wanted was a simple life. Just the normal things – a wife and kids who loved him, growing his arboreal business, contributing to community and country, time for fun and helping others. Chad laughed quietly to himself as he realized that what he wanted was what his parents had – right down to church on Sunday and big family dinners afterward. The American Dream! Chad glanced over at Mary Jo. So how did he ever get mixed up with this radical liberal with the blue lips and the sinister Uncle?

Mary Jo sucked furiously at the empty bottle. She moaned pathetically and began to struggle against the seat belt.

"It's okay, Mary Jo," Chad soothed her. "Calm down. There's plenty of kool-aid. I'll get you another bottle."

"What am I hearing?" thought Chad as he reached into the back seat and felt around for the cooler. "Must be a radio back here."

"Can't scratch fever . . .

They give me can't scratch fever . . . MEOW!"

Chad's searching hand came into contact with what felt like someone's bare butt. And maybe some other parts . . .

"Whoa there, sport," said a voice. Chad realized it hadn't been a radio, but someone singing. He snatched his hand back as a figure in the backseat sat up. "No handling the merchandise," laughed the voice. Chad looked in the rear view mirror and gasped.

"Naughty Ned, the Auto City Wildman!" yelled Chad happily. "Is this all a dream? Or a nightmare? I mean, come on, now – this is really out there. *You!* In my backseat! With no pants on! Where's your pants, Ned?"

"Sorry to shoot you down, sport," replied Ned. "This is no dream. Too far out for you?" he asked. "It's the no pants thing, right? Well, you know the song. Don't worry about the pants, sport. Just helps to air out the bits and pieces, cool down the fever. Can't scratch, you know. Love them kitties, but I pay the price. I'll put 'em back on before I go topside. OW! Just sat on an arrow! Guess I'll put them on now and sort out these weapons."

"Weapons? Are you taking us hostage? What's going on?"

"Moe didn't tell you, did he? HA! That's a good one. Played a little joke on us both, didn't he?" Ned laughed. "*ALRIGHT!* The game is *on*! Maybe I'll borrow the Posie fat suit and give him a real scare," chuckled Ned as he pulled on his pants. "But that's for later. Right now we've got other fish to fry. Things are about to get real hairy, real quick."

"What do you mean, Ned?" asked Chad. "I thought all we had to do was drive to the border, get into Alaska and meet up with . . . you know who."

"Well, it ain't no Sunday stroll in the park, sport," said Ned. "We're in the wilds of Canada and you're about to see what makes it so wild. There's weird things in these parts, so I'm along to ride shotgun. Where is that blasted shotgun, anyway? I've got rifles, pistols, special guns and ammo, longbows, crossbows, compound bows, tranq guns, arrows up the wazoo, grenades, claymores, rocket launcher, bazooka, napalm. No shotgun and that'll probably be just what I need. Thought it was in here."

"Gee, Ned, you must have raided an armory!"

"No need, I just emptied out my hall closet. Looks like Sleeping Beauty there is waking up," Ned said as he swapped out Mary Jo's empty for a full bottle. "Okay, I'm going topside. You just drive, I'll handle the incoming."

"Incoming what?" Chad wondered nervously as he concentrated on the road ahead. "How can this trip possibly get any weirder?"

He was about to find out.

Chapter 11
Into The Weird

"DONT'T MAKE EYE CONTACT! DON'T MAKE EYE CONTACT!" Ned yelled at Chad. "DRIVE RIGHT OVER THEM!"

"But," Chad protested, "the small one is wearing pearls. And the other one is old and has glasses . . ."

"RUN THEM OVER IF I MISS," yelled Ned. "Don't you know who they are?"

"I see a couple of huge rats," replied Chad. "As big as people. With pearls. And glasses. They look harmless enough, like grand-parents." Chad drove closer. "Scary grandparents." Chad slowed the car and the rats advanced. "OH MY GOD," Chad screamed. "That's . . ."

"NAZI AND DINGY!" Ned yelled as he sprayed them with bullets. Chad drove over the bodies.

"I've got to admit," he said, "I liked driving over those two. They've done it enough to me and mine." Chad smiled grimly. "So now someone reasonable who puts country and American citizens first will replace them?" he asked Ned.

"Not exactly," replied Ned. "Stop here for a minute. We're safe for awhile." Ned pushed a button and his hunting chair automati-cally descended into the backseat and the roof of the Cougar closed. "We can't totally get rid of them up here. This, sport, the wilds of Canada, is where they can be their dirty rotten corrupt slimy true selves. In the U.S. of A., they put on pretty faces and smooth, lying voices and free barbeque. They make promises, court special interest groups and pit brother against brother, when it should be us against them. They're wiping their butts with the Constitution and borrowing us into slavery. They've been fooling the people, lying to the people, stealing from the people and generally screwing the people. Then they hide up here in Canada and morph into their avatars, so you'll see some weird stuff here. It's become a real vacation hot spot for them! You know, sport, if their constituents saw them for what they really are, and realized what they're really doing, they'd be voted out in a Dee-troit minute! Until the people ignore their lying words and smiling faces and look at facts and reason, until America wakes up, they'll remain in power. But people *are* waking up, sport." Ned kicked the back of the driver's seat. *"People are waking up!"*

"Yeah, okay, I heard you," said Chad. "People are waking up."

"Your girlfriend, sport, she's *waking up*. She needs a refill. You better keep an eye on that, you *do not* want her to hit empty," stated Ned emphatically. "I've been around groupies zonked out on drugs, but nothing that was as heavy duty as this blue pill kool-aid. Look at her – brain and legs and mouth wide open – anything at all can get in, and probably has." Ned glanced at Chad. "Sounds harsh, sport. Sorry. A lot of good people become out-of-control groupies. Out-of-their-own-control, I mean."

Mary Jo writhed and thrashed. "No-no-no-no . . ." she moaned. Suddenly she scrunched up her face and began a pathetic mewling.

Chad quickly replaced the empty with a full bottle. Mary Jo quieted and sucked contentedly.

"So she's a groupie, huh?" Chad asked.

"You bet she is," replied Ned. "It's that cult-of-personality thing. Rock star, movie star, political star – we've all got groupies and in their eyes we can do no wrong. So it's up to the rock star, movie star or political star to act responsibly when it comes to groupies. What power does a rock or movie groupie have? The power to buy a concert or movie ticket, CD or DVD . . . not really a lot. The political star's groupies, though, have the power to vote. But they willingly, mindlessly turn that power over to the star to control. They vote how they're told, they feel they don't have to think and reason about the issues because they trust their star, and they get a warm fuzzy feeling too."

Ned pushed a button and the Cougar's roof opened. "Let's roll, sport," he said. "Those rats will be good as new and really mad when they come to."

"But . . ." Chad began.

"No time for buts, sport – INCOMING!" Ned yelled as his hunting chair ascended into battle.

Chapter 12
Even Weirder

"What *are* those things?" Chad asked as the latest onslaught subsided and Ned dropped back into the vehicle. "I've never seen anything like these before."

"Don't you recognize any of their faces?" Ned asked him. "Maybe from election posters or TV? These, sport, are some of our elected and appointed office holders! See how they come in all different sizes? The biggest ones are feds, then they get smaller on down the hierarchy. Now I said some, not all. There are some in office who are fighting for the people, problem is, they're few and far between"

"They're horrible," said Chad. "They look like . . . I don't know what!" Chad was stunned as he thought about what he'd seen.

"That's my job," Ned grinned. "I know predators! These are some of the worst. Look at those teeth and claws. And they're fast – you wouldn't believe how fast they can get what they want. Sneaky, too. You don't know what they're really doing because they're making a big noise about something else. Then by the time you figure it out, it's too late, they've screwed us over again. They love themselves and give themselves presents and expect everyone else to give them presents too. Their primary, no, their *only* motivation is to get themselves re-elected or re-appointed."

"You're right, I can't believe how fast they are," said Chad, "what with them being so close to the ground. What sort of a body is that? A weasel? A skunk? A mink?"

"All of the above and then some," laughed Ned, "but the chassis is pure honey badger, the most dangerous animal known to man. Robert Ruark (look him up, sport) said the honey badger has a lot in common with the modern American woman – they both go straight for the groin!" Ned winced. "This is the political version. It goes straight for your wallet! And they're close to the ground so they can wallow in the swill and dig themselves a hole to hide in when the people object to their actions."

"I don't understand why Canada puts up with all this. They should root out this mess!" Chad was indignant.

"It's *our* mess, sport, they just hide here. And other places all over the world, like villas, haciendas, mansions, estates," said Ned. "But we're watching and learning where they hide. We'll hunt them down one by one, eliminate their avatars and vote their sorry butts out of office! Besides, Canadians have the government-run health plan. Mostly they try not to get sick or hurt so they don't have to deal with their nightmare system. And they're busy saving what money they can so they can afford to travel to the U.S. if they have something serious and don't want to die waiting. Do you see any Canadians around here, anyway? *Wilds of Canada,* sport!"

Ned used the periscope to scout their surroundings. "I guess we'll move on," he said. "I wouldn't want us to get stuck at night in this next part, but I think we can make it. The sooner we get that red pill into her, the better."

"I'm not going to even ask what's ahead of us," said Chad.

"It wouldn't matter if you did," said Ned. "You wouldn't believe it until you see it!" Ted laughed. "Lighten up, sport, it's an adventure. It's epic! People will write songs about it. You're the *hero*, you're rescuing the damsel in distress. Why so glum, Beowulf?"

"I don't feel like a hero," admitted Chad. "I'm starting to feel like a lot of this is *my* fault. Mine, and other people like me. We didn't make the best choices in elections or make sure the candidates shared our values. We didn't protect our freedoms." Chad glanced at Mary Jo. "*My fault* . . ."

"INCOMING!" Ned yelled happily, grinning as only the Wildman can. "Light 'em up!" And he ascended into battle once again.

Chapter 13
And Weirder

"**S**TOP!" yelled Ned. Chad slammed on the brakes.

"What is it?" asked Chad. "What do you see?"

"Step on up here, sport, take a look." Chad joined him and Ned handed him the field glasses.

"I still don't know what it is," said Chad. "It's sure covering a lot of ground. Is it moving? Is it growing? What *is* it? Kind of a green vine? Is it kudzu? You know, 'the vine that ate the South'?"

"No," Ned replied, "but that's a good guess. It's actually Gorezu, kind of a cousin of kudzu. It's growing and spreading and trying to cover the United States. It's got cap and trade in it, Imoult's Government Electric, Government Motor's clown cars, graft and corruption, Cash for Junkers and the Copenhagen Treaty and lobbyists and all kinds of junk. All kinds of expensive, too. It can turn our country into a Banana Republic."

"But Mary Jo says our carbon emissions are destroying the planet and we need to . . ."

"Yeah, sport, and your girlfriend's such a reliable source, right? She's repeating talking points! I bet she's clueless about the truth. Sure, we have climate change and we always will. But the real science shows something different than what's projected by the government. Do you know that if the entire United States stopped using carbon-based fuel – and I mean totally stopped, no cars, no industry, no electricity, not even a campfire – in *thirty-*

three years, the earth's mean temperature would decrease by only one degree! Seriously, sport, this is a bad, bad thing. It needs to be killed."

"What'll you do? Use a mine? A grenade?" asked Chad.

"Nope. I haven't got the kind of firepower that could take that out," said Ned. "A nuke, maybe, but not permanently. The voters have to pressure it out of existence. Let's see if we can find a route around it. I'll figure this out, you might want to freshen up your girlfriend there. I think a change of Depends might be in order."

Chad got Mary Jo's seat belt unbuckled and went to the back of the vehicle to get the Depends. All of a sudden he noticed movement near Mary Jo's open door and a weird tableau presented itself.

Chad was stopped dead in his tracks. "Santa!" he thought, but before the thought was even complete he realized something was terribly wrong. Santa wore a ball cap and thick black-framed glasses. Instead of a beard, his fat jowls were covered with dark stubble. He was so fat his red suit was splitting and greenish scum was oozing out. His sleigh was a chopped and cropped old ambulance and the two 'reindeer' pulling it looked a lot like Santa, only somewhat smaller and with their heads stuck firmly up their own butts. And even worse, Santa was luring Mary Jo towards the sleigh!

"Would you like some kool-aid, little girl?" cooed Santa. "Sure you would. You're so thirsty, and only icy cool, bright blue kool-aid will quench your thirst."

Mary Jo took another step and reached for Santa's outstretched hand. Her eyes were open and her blue lips were smiling.

"NO," yelled Chad. "NED! Santa's taking Mary Jo!"

"That's not Santa!" Ned yelled as Santa whisked Mary Jo away in the sleigh. "That's . . ."

Chapter 14
Kidnapped Again

"Look at this!" Ned waved the empty bottle at Chad, then threw it to the side of the road. "Pick that up," he told Chad. "We don't litter! I told you not to let her run dry. If she'd been passed out, he wouldn't have got her." Ted kicked at the ground. "Sorry, sport, don't mean to snap at you. This is just really, really bad. Now what? We're gonna need reinforcements."

He took out a phone and dialed. "The specimen's been taken. Pickup and reinforcements needed ASAP. She's bugged, so you can track her. Okay, 15 minutes." He turned to Chad. "We'll get her back. Help is on the way. Get your gear together, don't leave anything that can ID you."

"But who took her? Who was that in the Santa suit? What does he want with her and where is he taking her?" Chad had too many questions and his head was spinning.

"Slow down, sport. Take a break. Here, have some water. Have some jerky. I made it myself. Got to keep your strength up. Can't fight the bad guys without fueling up once in awhile." Ned chewed on his own piece of jerky.

"So that Santa was a bad guy?" Chad asked.

"Of course he was a bad guy! Did you see that rig?" Ned snapped. "Sorry. I need to *SHOOT SOMETHING*," he yelled, then took a deep breath. "That, sport, was a giant slab of pond scum that goes by the name of Mikhail Smore. You may have heard of him.

America-hating, Bush-bashing, commie-loving, money-grubbing, fact-twisting Mikhail Smore. None other. Your blue-lipped baby doll is firmly in the bad guy's clutches." Ned sighed heavily. "I should have seen a trap. That Gorezu was way too far north for this time of year."

"Mikhail Smore?" asked Chad. "What would he want with Mary Jo? And what were those things pulling his sleigh?"

"Those *things*," Ned told him, "are *him*. Smore thinks nationalized healthcare countries have better care than the U.S., so he set out to prove it. Nugo Ravage offered to clone the stupid slob for free. Now Smore can't get rid of them."

"But why would Mikhail Smore take Mary Jo?" Chad still wanted to know.

"He must be working for someone. That's the only answer. He's delivering her to someone else. Believe me, from what I've heard of Mikhail Smore's anatomy, he'd have absolutely no use for your girlfriend's special talents." Ned glanced over at Chad. "Sorry, sport, I meant her . . . er . . . blogging talents. Sure. Her *blogging* talents."

"Here's our ride," said Ned as a helicopter hovered above them. "Let's roll."

Chapter 15
Red Rider Revisited

"Eeuuwww . . . what's that smell?" said Mary Jo. "Are these sacks of *GARBAGE* I'm sitting on? You're not Santa, you're some *freak* who's kidnapped me! HELP! HELP!" she yelled. "Why are we flying? GET ME DOWN FROM HERE! Oh no! Your reindeer are disgusting! *HELP*!"

"Now, now, princess, I have kool-aid! All will be well." He fumbled in the garbage bag beside him. He pulled out an old sippy cup with a pale blue warm liquid inside. "Drink up!"

Mary Jo took the cup and looked at it suspiciously. She shook the cup. She poured a few drops into her hand. She sniffed the liquid, smiled and took a big gulp.

"Bleech," she gagged, spitting out the stuff. "You call that kool-aid? That's gross and disgusting, just like you! I want to go home! I want Chad! I want my special kool-aid! I want my bottle! I want my Depends changed! Waaaahhhh," Mary Jo wailed. She threw the sippy cup at Smore. It broke open and kool-aid covered his head and dripped down onto the Santa suit.

"THAT'S ENOUGH OF THAT," he yelled at Mary Jo. "You behave or I'll . . ." Mary Jo stuck her blue tongue out and wiggled it at him. "Okay, okay, just put that thing away," Mikhail shuddered. "Crap," he muttered. "They swore this was uncut, and I only stepped on it a little, teeny tiny bit. I'm screwed. She's gonna freak out over not having the good stuff and I'll wind up called onto the carpet over this."

"Uncle, Uncle," Mary Jo whimpered, sucking her thumb.

"Look, we're gonna have to make an unscheduled stop. We'll get you some better kool-aid. We;ll get you cleaned up and you'll be all pretty for your date. You'll see, everything will be fine." Mikhail whispered to himself. "Everything will be just fine." He rooted through a garbage bag and pulled out a phone.

"*PHONE!*" Mary Jo shrieked like a banshee and launched herself toward the precious object. She clawed at Smore's hand, grabbed the phone and . . . oops . . . over the side it went, tumbling to earth below.

"You idiot!" Mikhail reached back and tried to get his hands around Mary Jo's neck. "I'm gonna squeeze the kool-aid right out of you." At the mention of kool-aid, Mary Jo went limp and moaned. Smore released his grip.

"AARRGGHH!" Mary Jo yelled in triumph and tried to claw his eyes out. Smore began hitting her with his garbage bag. "Land this thing RIGHT NOW!" Mary Jo demanded.

"I can't!" Mikhail yelled back. "You stupid fool . . . you lost the phone!"

"Whatever. Just tell your disgusting . . . just tell *those things* to land this wreck!" Mary Jo banged his head against the steering wheel. "GET ME DOWN!"

"I can't," Mikhail yelled again. "LOOK AT THEM! Their heads are up their asses! I can only reach them by phone, and YOU THREW AWAY THE PHONE!"

Chapter 16
Losing Control

"This is really disgusting," mumbled Mary Jo, as she sucked the kool-aid off of Mikhail Smore's earlobe.

"Yesss," moaned Mikhail, "it is disgusting. I think there's some deep inside that ear." He looked anything but disgusted.

"You're disgusting too, you jerk, but I meant your – whatever it is that's pulling us. That one on the left just took another flying crap. But their heads are up their asses, where's it come from? They don't eat. Do they eat their insides?" Mary Jo sighed. "I just wish I had some kool-aid. You jerk." And she smacked him upside the head.

"The crap comes from their brains," he explained. "Maybe things weren't as Sickly as I thought, I don't know why I trusted Nugo Ravage. Well, Brawn Penncil told me to. That little weasel. Then they swore Cuba was the best place to do it. Now I'm stuck with them. I can't get rid of them. I've tried. No one wants them – not Nugo, not Brawn, not the Mastro brothers, not even Octo-mom!"

"We've got to find a phone," said Mary Jo, frantically digging through the trash. She'd opened many of the garbage bags earlier, looking for kool-aid. "What *is* all this junk? Why are you carrying garbage around with you?" She ripped open another bag.

"That's not garbage," replied Smore, "that's my life."

"Life! *YOUR* life!" shrieked Mary Jo. "What about *MY* life, you moron! You kidnap me, you're gross and disgusting. You promised me kool-aid and you don't have any!" Mary Jo ripped open more bags and started throwing junk out of the ambulance. "You took my life away, now I'm taking yours!"

"Wait, wait, wait . . . don't throw that stuff out! You're looking for kool-aid and maybe there's some in a pocket or . . . and we might need that stuff if we're stuck up here. I have an idea! A way to get down! Don't throw it out," Mikhail pleaded.

"AARRGGHH!" Mary Jo screamed and threw a tantrum. She stomped her feet and kicked at the back of Smore's seat. She banged her head against a garbage bag. She shrieked her rage and pummeled the bags. "Why me? Why'd you take *me?*"

"Calm down, calm down . . . I'll tell you. You're important. Well, you actually aren't important at all." Mary Jo kicked the back of his seat. "Wait, wait, it's that someone important wants to meet you so that makes *you* important too!

"I meet people all the time. They don't need to kidnap me," said Mary Jo sullenly.

"No, I know, they just needed to keep it really, *really* secret. I'm not supposed to tell you this, but you made me, okay, you made me tell you, remember that if anyone asks. They want to thank you, you know, for the work. The blogging and stuff." Mikhail risked a glance into the rear view mirror to see if she was buying it.

"Wow!" Mary Jo brightened visibly. "They know about me?! Who are they? How do I look? When will we get there?" Mary Jo fluffed her hair and moistened her blue lips.

"Slow down, toots," said Mikhail. "In case you've forgotten, we're up in the air without a phone."

"Didn't you say you had a way to get down?" Mary Jo's eyes narrowed and glittered angrily.

"Yeeessss . . . ," Mikhail moaned unhappily. "I guess I did."

Chapter 17
Into the Fray

"**H**ope you're a good shot, sport," said Ned, handing Chad the M1. "Give this baby a try. Only gun you can actually lock and load, lock back the bolt and load the clip from the top. Just pretend you're at the carnival, sport! I'm gonna go Desert Eagle on 'em." He picked up the huge .50 caliber pistol.

"Whoa, there," Ted yelled as Chad aimed. "Don't shoot those Red Dog Republicans! You know what they say about a red dog – scrappiest, feistiest dog in the yard. Gets something between his teeth and won't let go. Look at those two there – they've got the thieving badgers on the run. Hold your fire! Don't shoot those Blue Dog Democrats, either – they're fiscally responsible and against big spending. They can put the brakes on their runaway party any time they want."

"Better get your finger off the trigger, Ned," said the pilot. "And buckle in before you fire that hogleg," he continued. "Shoot that thing while I'm dodging enemy fire and the recoil could blow you out the other door!"

"Yes sir, Big Rushbo, my man," Ned replied. He and Chad quickly buckled in. "Nobody draws fire like you. Even the top guy in the White House takes a shot at Big Rushbo!"

"There's a cooler behind you, guys, full of red meat. Open it up and throw it to those Red Dogs. We like to give them lots of tasty tidbits to sink their teeth into," said Big Rushbo.

"What kind of tidbits?" asked Chad. "By the way," he said, "I'm Chad Sixpack. Thank you for helping us."

"Helping you is helping the country, Chad," said Big Rushbo. "Make sure you toss that meat where the Red Dogs can see it," he said, "if those thieving badgers get to it first they'll dig a hole, bury it, cover it up. Then they'll all form a circle around it and swear it never happened and even if it did it wasn't them, it was all Bush's fault and they know nothing. See that big piece of meat they're trying to cover up now? That's WALNUT information, stuff that will start an investigation. Don't worry, the Red Dogs chased those thieving badgers off and have the meat."

"Go, Dogs," cheered Ned. "*LOOK OUT*," he yelled as another helicopter buzzed them.

"It's that crazy Heck." Big Rushbo calmly swooped away. "He'll do anything for a laugh, but he's busy getting the red meat out there, day after day. Along with Bill, Laura, Sean, Neil, Tammy, Mike . . . it's a *long* list!"

"Did you see who's riding with Heck today?" asked Ned. "I think I saw Ann, Michelle and Bernie. *YES*! Look at that! Would you look at the arm on our Annie! Way to go, Annie!" yelled Ned. "Uh oh – here we go!" Ned pulled his head back inside the helicopter.

"INCOMING!" he yelled.

Chapter 18
Loons Away

"Are those *people* riding those giant birds?" Chad asked.

"They're not *riding* the birds," said Ned. "And they're not people. Look close – they're *part* of the birds! We call them Left-Wing Loons."

"Why?" asked Chad. "It looks like they have two wings to me."

"It's because they only turn left," said Ned. "They're what used to be called mainstream media, now known as *lamestream* media. Watch, soon they'll start circling, like vultures. They smell the meat."

"They're circling! What now?" Chad found out soon enough. "OH NO, HELP!" Chad looked at the Red Dogs below. "We've got to help them! They're under attack! *We're* under attack!"

"Not to worry, sport," said Ned. "Take a closer look. It helps to squint, or try these field glasses," he said, handing them to Chad.

Chad followed his instructions. Instead of the carnage he'd expected, he saw that the Red Dogs were unharmed, although nearly obscured by gray clouds and flashes of bright light. "What *is* that?" he asked Ned.

"Smoke and mirrors, sport, smoke and mirrors! That's their big guns. That and their filth bombs – they fling the poo and hope something sticks," explained Ned.

"Look at the thieving badgers, they're using the smoke and mirrors too," said Big Rushbo. "They always do. We'll get rid of the loons and let the Dogs get back to work."

Chad grabbed his rifle.

"Not so fast, sport," said Ned. "There's an easier way, and we're in a hurry." He pointed at the horizon.

"That's Mancrow. That paint on his chopper is from paintball wars. Too bad Bratner's not with him – wait, he is!" Ned rubbed his palms together gleefully.

Bill Bratner leaned out of Mancrow's chopper. He had a paintball gun in his hand and a loon call between his lips. "Buusshhh!" he called, "Buusshhh!" The loons immediately became violent, scrambling madly to reach the hated sound. Since they could only turn left, there were many midair collisions. The Olberwoman and Matthscrews loons wound up in an extremely compromising position! They both felt tingles running up their drumsticks and instantly became non-combatants. Bratner pelleted the loons with red paint, all the time bugling his plaintive call, ":Buusshhh, Buusshhh!"

"That's . . . not natural," said Chad weakly. "What's wrong with them?"

"BDS, sport, Bush Derangement Syndrome. Watch what happens next," Ned chuckled.

Chad watched as Bratner brought a mannequin to the chopper's open bay. It wore a cowboy hat and cowboy boots and a sign was hung around it's neck. The sign said "BUSH" in big red letters.

"Bombs away," called Bratner, and dropped the effigy. It plummeted towards earth, followed closely by the shrieking loons. The Bush decoy hit the ground, and the loons nosedived after it. Soon there was a heap of shattered loons covering the effigy.

"Works every time!" exclaimed Ned. "Okay, let's get going, Big Rushbo, we've got a rescue mission ahead." Ned brought out a silver flash. "Care for a nip of moonshine, sport? I made it myself. Take a pull while I stow these guns. We won't need them for awhile."

Chad accepted the flask and took a large gulp. He felt the fire start in his belly and spread . . . and spread and spread. Chad took a deep breath and passed out.

"Damn!" said Ned. "Lost another one. Got to remember to cut it with water for these city boys!"

Chapter 19
If Barty Does It . . .

"You're sure Barty did this?" asked Mary Jo.

"Positive," said Mikhail, "didn't you read his book?"

Mary Jo firmly grasped the base of the object. She placed the head of the object in her mouth and wrapped her lips around it.

"Like this?" she mumbled at Mikhail.

"Yes," he said. "Well, no. You don't need to swallow it. Just put your lips to the opening." Mikhail applied a flame to the green material in the bowl. "Now inhale, princess," he told Mary Jo. "Beautiful, beautiful," he crooned. "Just like Barty. Now hold it in. I'll count for you. One buttmonkey, two buttmonkey, three butt-monkey, four buttmonkey . . ." Mikhail tried to take the bong from Mary Jo.

"NO," she screamed, billowing out a cloud of bright blue smoke. "*MINE*!" And she snatched it away greedily.

"*Yours*? No way, you greedy little bogarting bee-atch! I've put up with enough out of you. I've suffered. I've worked and worked on getting us down and my hands are blistered and I'm tired and you've pulled my hair and kicked me and punched me and screamed at me . . . I deserve a bong hit!" Mikhail shrieked angrily and made a desperate grab.

Mary Jo held the bong away from him. "Mine. Mine, mine, mine," she stated. She turned her back to Mikhail and took another bong hit. She held the smoke in. "It's . . . Barty's . . . he'd . . . want me . . . to . . . have it." She turned back to Mikhail and exhaled in his face. He greedily tried to suck in the bright blue smoke.

"You behave," Mary Jo told him, "and I'll blow the smoke your way. Otherwise, up, up and away it goes."

"Okay," said Mikhail. "You win. Any little bit. Go ahead, blow it my way!"

Time passed. And passed. And passed.

Mary Jo awoke, clutching the bong to her bosom. "Hey!" She kicked Smore in the head. "Hey, wake up!"

Mikhail snored on, his Ken doll clutched to his bosom. "Ken . . . pretty Kenny . . ." he muttered.

Mary Jo tried to light the bong, but there was nothing to burn. "Bummer," she moaned and shook the bong. "What's that smell? Could it be?" Mary Jo put her nose to the bong and inhaled. "Kool-aid! *Barty's* kool-aid! It was here all along!" She put her lips to the bong, tilted back her head and chugged the bong kool-aid. Her throat spasmed as she got her fix.

"AARRGGHH!" she yelled. "That's more like it!" She let out a huge belch and passed out on top of Mikhail, trapping the Ken doll between them.

Chapter 20
Smore Has More

Mary Jo leaned back in the passenger seat of the ambulance sleigh, her feet propped on the dash. "What *is* this crap I'm listening to?" she asked as she pulled the earbuds from her ears and tossed the ipod into the backseat.

"That's my top 666 playlist," said Mikhail Smore. He was tearing and braiding and fashioning a makeshift rope from the clothing in the garbage bags. "Don't you listen to Toe Jam, Chixie Tricks, Cant Evens . . .?"

"Yuck and double yuck," scowled Mary Jo.

"So what musical greats do you listen to?"

"Well, I wanted to only listen to artists named Barty," said Mary Jo, "but there aren't any! So I only listen to artists named *Barry*, 'cause that's really close to *Barty*. Barry White, Barry Manilow, Barry Canning, Barry Brown, Barry Bostwick . . . I like music by *anyone* named Barry!" she stated emphatically. "And once those morons pay attention to my emails, calls and letters and change their names to Barty, I'll like them even better! *Barty* White, *Barty* Manilow, *Barty* Canning, *Barty* Brown, *Barty* Bostwick . . ." she recited dreamily.

"Well, okaaaayyy . . .," said Mikhail, thinking furiously. "So you're really fond of Barty, and anything Barty does, right?

"Absolutely. If Barty does it, it's good, no doubt, no question." Mary Jo looked at him angrily. "I think everyone should just listen to Barty, he knows best!"

"Maybe so, princess, maybe so," said Smore, still thinking furiously. "Hand me that garbage bag on the driver's seat." Mary Jo complied. "I've got something of Barty's in here that I think you'd be interested in."

"Really?! Something of Barty's? Where did you get it? Why do you have it? Did you *steal* it from Barty?" Mary Jo's hands formed fists. "If you stole it, you better give it back to Barty and hope he doesn't put you in jail!"

"No, no, sweetness, he wouldn't put me in jail. I'm doing him a favor. I'm keeping it safe for him. You see, he can't keep it where he's at now, but he'll want it later," said Mikhail. "I'm sure he wouldn't mind if you saw it, though – you and him being so close and all."

"We are close," insisted Mary Jo. "I understand him and no one else does. I will protect him and keep him safe and I will attack all his enemies and he will be King of the World!" Mary Jo recited the words mechanically.

"There, there," said Mikhail. "I understand. You should calm down, though. I have an idea!" he said happily. "Barty would want you to calm down, and what with you being so close and all . . . he probably wouldn't mind if you saw this special thing of his that I'm keeping safe."

"We *are* close," Mary Jo insisted once again. "And we're going to be even closer. He just can't leave the First Hag yet, because of the children. He explained it all to me. But once they're older, and he's King for Life . . ." Mary Jo's eyes dreamed far into the future and she almost purred.

"That's great, that's just great. I'm so happy for you. Now that I know how things stand between you and Barty, I feel lots better about showing you this. This is very important to Barty, and it's very important that people who don't like what Barty's doing don't find out about this. But you . . . well, that's almost like Barty himself being here," said Mikhail. He dug through the garbage bag, grasped an object and withdrew it in triumph. "Just look at this!" he exclaimed.

Mary Jo frowned. "Barty does woodcarving?" she wondered.

"No," chortled Mikhail, waving the life-size wooden hand in triumph, "this is The Bird Of Power!"

"Oh!" Mary Jo exclaimed brightly, "because it's middle finger is flipping the Bird!"

"Exacta-rooney, sweetness," said Mikhail, "but remember, it's all hush-hush for now. Barty has a special place in the O Office all cleared off for this, he's just waiting for the right time to display it. And he hasn't got the spotlight for it installed yet. It's all top, *top* secret. The people can't find out that this is his gift to them until it's too late. No, forget I said that. I mean the people can't know about this until the time is right because it's a *surprise* for them!"

"Barty can count on me," said Mary Jo solemnly, her hand over her alleged heart.

Chapter 21
Meet the Paines

"No . . ." muttered Chad. "Go 'way."

"Up and at 'em, sport. We're here and we've got work to do." Ned shook Chad again.

"Okay . . . okay, I'm awake. Where are we?" Chad asked.

"Still in the wilds of Canada," said Ned. "We're gonna meet some folks, get us a battle plan and reinforcements."

Big Rushbo landed the chopper. Ned and Chad prepared to exit.

"You're not coming with us?" asked Chad.

"No," said Big Rushbo. "Got to get back up there and hit the airwaves – keep the people informed."

"Thanks," said Chad, "and thanks for helping us."

"We all do what we can," said Big Rushbo. The helicopter rose into the sky.

Ned led the way to a small, neat red brick house. They piled their gear to the side and Ned knocked on the door.

"Come in," a voice called, "we're in the parlor."

Ned and Chad entered. "This way," said Ned, obviously familiar with the house. They entered the parlor. A man in Colonial garb stood to greet them.

"Tom, sorry to barge in on you like this. And so sorry to interrupt your evening, ma'am," Ned said to a figure lying on a fainting couch. "I'd like you to meet my good friend, Chad Sixpack."

"Chad, I'm glad we have the chance to meet, even under such undesirable and desperate circumstances. I'm Thomas Paine, and this is my bride, Common Sense." Paine gestured towards the fainting couch. The frail figure ensconced there gave a small wave and fainted.

"Thomas Paine!" exclaimed Chad. "It's such an honor to meet you. And you . . ." he began, turning to the couch. He turned back to Paine. "Pardon me, sir, I don't mean to be rude . . . but your wife . . . ah, I heard that Common Sense was dead." Chad blushed.

Paine smiled sadly. "Well, it's true she's not in the best of health. She's much better than she was, though. I will admit, there were times I thought she wouldn't make it. We almost lost her this last election cycle. People took leave of her in droves and elected that. . ." he leaned closer to Chad and whispered, ". . . community agitator! I understand your . . .er, how shall I put this delicately? . . . your *paramour* . . . is a fan of his."

"Oh, yes." said Chad. "He said he was a moderate, and that appealed to her."

Thomas Paine looked sternly at Chad. "*Those words, temperate and moderate, are words either of political cowardice, or of cunning, or seduction. A thing, moderately good is not so good as it ought to be. Moderation in temper, is always a virtue; but moderation in principle, is a species of vice.*"

"C'mon, Tom, lighten up." Ned punched his arm lightly. "Things are looking up, people are waking up, seeing where he and his lefty loony pals are taking the country and they're not liking it. No, they are not liking it at all. And when the people wake up, *she'll* wake up. Common Sense will return!" Ned said happily. "Oh, man, do you think she'll make those little pastry things with the strawberry jam when she wakes up?" asked Ned. "I sure could go for some of those. It's been a long time since she's been awake enough to make them." Ned's stomach rumbled.

"Pardon my inattention to guests, sirs. Please, step into the dining room. Supper is laid out and we will have company soon." Thomas Paine led the way.

Chapter 22
Nanny State

"AARRGGHH!" screamed Mary Jo. "Take that, you hick!" And she threw her soggy Depends onto a woman pushing a baby carriage below. The Depends rolled off the woman's head and into the carriage. "Wake up, you slug," she screamed in Mikhail's ear, "I just diaper- bombed Rogue Peyton!"

Mikhail looked below. He took off his glasses, cleaned them on his filthy shirt, put them back on and looked again. "You moron! That's not Rogue Peyton. Now we're in for it. Oh no, no, no . . . my life just gets worse and worse. YOU," he pointed at Mary Jo. "*YOU* ruined my life! I am a respected filmmaker, a noted talk show guest . . ."

"Is that you, Mikhail Smore, you filthy freak?" yelled a voice from the ground. "Look what you did! What the hell is the matter with you?"

"Sorry, Sabine," Mikhail called. "It was an accident. My, uh, passenger was putting it in the trash when she dropped it. Are you okay? Is that Hal Hanken in the baby carriage?"

"That's right," Sabine called back. "How dare she treat a new U.S. Senator like that?" She removed the Depends from Hanken's face and threw it on the ground. "There, there, Hal, baby," she cooed as she wiped his face, adjusted his glasses, straightened his baby bonnet and checked his diaper for wetness or worse. She popped the nipple of a baby bottle containing bright blue liquid between his lips. "Did that nasty redneck racist upset my widdle Hankie-ums?"

"WAAHH," wailed Hal. "Smore," he mumbled, "meanie."

"Yes Hankie, he is a big old meanie-weenie," said Sabine. "I remember what he did to you when you passed out at my party."

"Teabagged me," wailed Hal. "Didn't wanna pass out! He drugged me!"

"I know, Hankie, I know." Sabine wiped his nose. "It was my fault . . . all my fault. I should have kept an eye on you. I knew how much Mikhail liked you, but I didn't know he liked you *that* way. Can you ever forgive me?" she pleaded.

"Make him pay," said Hal coldly. "Make him wish he'd never been born."

"I will, Hankie, I will," promised Sabine. "He'll pay for tea-bagging my widdle Hankie-kins." She looked up at the flying ambulance. "You! Smore! Get your lard ass down here pronto," she demanded. "I've got a bone to pick with you and I want to beat the crap out of your redneck racist passenger for throwing that Depends! What the hell was she doing and who did that thing belong to?"

"Ah, sorry, Sabine," Mikhail called back. "No can do. My phone got . . . he glared at Mary Jo . . . dropped. Can't contact Tweedledeedumb and Tweedledeedumber. Sweetness here dropped the Depends on you because she thought you were Rogue Peyton. It was a simple case of mistaken identity. She's really, *really* sorry. We're kind of stuck up here, can you help us out?"

"Rogue Peyton!" Sabine shrieked. "*Rogue Peyton*! My God, don't I look bad enough? Can't you tell I'm not that horrible, horrible person? I guess I *don't* look bad enough! Well, I'll fix that, Mr. Teabagging Smore!" She pulled scissors out of her diaper bag and began to chop off her hair. "How could you think I was her? Look, look, I can be uglier than this! I can be just as ugly on the outside as I am on the inside! Watch this!" And she began to hack her hair off. Soon she had tufts of black hair sticking out from a bloody scalp. "Look at this, you bozo!" She scratched at her face with long jagged nails. "Look here! And you know it's gonna scab over and *really* look bad! So there! Look how ugly I am now! No one will ever, ever mistake me for her ever again!" she screamed. "Get you down?! You bet your fat ass I'll get you down! I'll get a gun and SHOOT YOU DOWN!"

"Now, Sabine," called Mikhail. "You know we don't like the Second Amendment!"

Chapter 23
First Aid

"Hey there, princess," called Mikhail, "no need to moon the birdies!"

Mary Jo was standing in the backseat, leaning over the passenger seat. The breeze had blown her skirt above the waist. "My butt hurts," she said. "I think I have a rash."

Mikhail reluctantly glanced over at her butt. "Yuck!" he exclaimed. "I think it's diaper rash. Gross! It's all over!" He quickly turned away.

"So what do I do about it?" asked Mary Jo.

"Look in those bags, there's got to be some kind of ointment or something. You can borrow a pair of my boxers," Mikhail told her. Mary Jo rummaged through the bags.

She found ointment and a pair of the boxers. "No way," she said in disgust, throwing the boxers over the side. They landed on Hanken, who quickly hid them under his pillow, along with the discarded Depends he'd slyly retrieved. She dove back into the bags. With some papers, the ointment, duct tape and a couple of Ace bandages, Mary Jo managed to put her butt in a sling.

Mikhail leaned over the side of the ambulance sleigh and called to Sabine. "Sabine . . .," he cried plaintively, "please, just look for my phone down there. It's important! You gotta believe me, you know I don't lie to my friends – well, not much. It's important! It's for the country, and all. It's for the LIBERAL AGENDA!!! If you're really as far left as you say you are, you HAVE TO HELP ME!" Smore demanded.

Sabine looked up and flipped him off.

Mary Jo leaned over the side in time to see it. "Look at that witch!" she said. "Look at that big baby." She began to hyperventilate. "HE'S . . . GOT . . . MY . . . KOOL-AID . . . BOTTLE!!!" she screamed, then she began to wail. "WAAHH, WAAHH, WAAHH! I WANT MY BOTTLE!"

Mikhail tried to shush her. "Quiet, you moron! We need their help! If we can get them to help us, we'll get you the really, really good kool-aid. Just shut up now. Shhh . . . hush up right this minute!"

Mary Jo quieted and began to hiccup softly. Her thumb sneaked into her mouth and she stared intently at the bottle below. She sucked furiously and her eyes fluttered.

"Sabine!" Mikhail yelled excitedly. "There it is! Look-look-look . . . right in front of the carriage! Don't drive over it!"

Sabine stopped the carriage and picked up the phone.

"Thank you, Sabine, oh, thank you, thank you!" Mikhail slobbered. "Just push that big blue button there and talk into the clown's mouth. Tweedledeedumb and Tweedledeedumber will hear you and do what you tell them. Now, I want you to tell them to go . . ."

Sabine cut him off. "Better buckle up," she said. "It's gonna be a bumpy ride." She chuckled evilly.

"Sabine, no . . . please-please-please no," he pleaded while scrambling to buckle his seat belt, knowing full well what she was going to do. "This is *important*, really, *really* important. You help and you'll get invites to all the important big time political parties. I promise! I have connections, you know I do! Important people are waiting for her," he glanced at Mary Jo, still in her trance-like state. He shook her. "Wake up, princess, wake up! Put that seat belt on!" Mary Jo continued to suck her thumb and gaze at the bottle below. "Sabine," he yelled angrily, "if she gets hurt, we're both dead meat!"

Sabine pushed the blue button on the phone. "Now where was it you wanted to go, Mikhail?" she asked sweetly.

"Thank you, Sabine, thank you," said Mikhail, while taking the precaution of buckling Mary Jo in her seat. "I have to take her to . . . EEEEEEKKK!!!" he screamed as the wild ride began.

Chapter 24
Playtime

"Didn't you hear about Barty's Cash for Junkers program?" gasped Mary Jo as the ambulance took off trailing a cloud of blue smoke. "It's polluting wrecks like this they want to get off the highways."

"Right, well, sweetness, just keep on believing whatever they tell you, but in case you haven't noticed, we *are* off the highways! Hold on!" Mikhail yelled as the sleigh began to twist and turn.

Far below, Sabine poured her evil instructions into the phone's clown mouth. "Up, down, sideways, drop thirty feet in a corkscrew," she said and sent them on a wild ride.

Meanwhile, Hanken was busy talking on his phone. "Okay, Sabine," he said. "Enough. I just checked out his story. He's to take her to The Cottage."

Sabine continued whispering into the clown's mouth as the sleigh rode an invisible roller coaster in the sky.

"Sabine!" Hanken yelled. "No more. They want her ASAP!"

She covered the clown's mouth with her hand. "Will you just give me a second?" she scowled. "I'm almost done." She sent the sleigh through it's final swoops and loops before bringing it to a halt in the sky.

Hanken looked up and began to laugh. There, in blue exhaust smoke, Sabine had spelled out:

TEABAGGERS SUCK!

He quickly snapped a phone photo. "Good one, Sabine! This one goes on my *private* office wall!"

"Yeah, that'll show those redneck racist Tea Party fools! Go ahead and have your parties, it doesn't matter. WE WON!" Sabine yelled and pumped her fist at the sky. "Too bad there aren't any Tea Party people here to see this!"

"They'll see it, Sabine, it'll be all over youtube in an hour," said Hanken, as he sent the image from his phone.

"That's great, Hankie! Did I hear you right? You said they're going to . . . ?" She waited.

"To The Cottage," said Hal, "and quick. They were supposed to be there an hour ago."

"You're kidding, right? Why would those two use Smore to do something like that? Surely they know that he'd bungle it. And what the heck do they want that little Depends-throwing twit for? Wait, it's those blue lips, isn't it? *Someone* wants those blue lips. Why don't they ever want MY lips, Hankie? Oh no, it's always "'just drop the slut off, Sabine, and be on your merry way'," she continued.

"Well, I happen to know that the big dummy up there gets violently seasick. So lets just give him a little boat ride! Time to ride the waves, Mikhail," she called up to the sleigh. The sleigh headed north, swooping up and down, up and down, up and down. Soon Smore was puking into one of the garbage bags.

"Enough, Sabine," yelled Hanken. "Control yourself!"

Sabine sighed and complied. "Okay, but you're not being any fun anymore, Hankie – not since you got to be a senator!"

"I explained all that," he replied. "I have to look serious and sober and work on my reelection. That's the name of the game. Five years service and I get full benefits and a free ride from the

American fools – er, I mean the American *citizens*, for life! And what's not to like about the job? Dinners, trips, freebies, people fawning over me, over a million in petty cash and I don't even have to read the bills, just vote the party line. I am a member of the most exclusive club in the world and I'm going to milk it for all it's worth and keep my butt in that seat until I'm a hundred! In case you didn't notice, Congress is America's aristocracy!"

"Okay," said Sabine, "explanation noted. Let's get them on their way. Destination – The Cottage. ETA – 30 minutes. Are you happy now, my widdle Hankie-wankie-ums?" she asked as she tucked him in.

Chapter 25

Suppertime

"**Y**ankee Doodle went to D.C.

　Just to kick their bu-utts

　Stuck a feather in his cap

　And threw out all the nu-uts!"

Ned sang quietly while waiting for the promised company. Chad sat dozing in a chair. They'd dined on a hearty spread that included venison roast ("I shot it myself," said Ned), creamed pheasant ("Them, too" said Ned), Tipsy Parson and Spotted Dick ("If you shot that too, I don't want to know about it," said Chad). Now the table was cleared and laid out with whiskey, wine, coffee and cookies. ("Bachelor Buttons!" Ned had exclaimed happily, "Thomas Jefferson's favorite!")

They heard a commotion at the front door and rose to greet the newcomers.

"Jon Voight! Kelsey Grammer!" Chad exclaimed. "What are you doing here?"

"Uh, sport," whispered Ned, "these guys are the real deal, not actors." He stepped forward. "President Washington, General Patton, sirs, may I present Chad Sixpack, boyfriend of Mary Jo. We need your help, sirs. Mary Jo's been recruited and is hooked on the blue pill kool-aid. Chad was taking her north to Rogue Peyton to get the red pill. The Red Mutt beer truck cover was blown and I was brought in to guide them the rest of the way. Unfortunately,

Mary Jo was kidnapped by Mikhail Smore. We don't know why, or where he's taking her. We've got GPS on her, so . . ."

"No need," General Patton interrupted. "Look!" He pointed to the window. They saw the words "TEABAGGERS SUCK" spelled out in blue exhaust smoke in the sky. "I think we can assume that's them. That Sabine witch and Hanken must be in control. Smore would never subject himself to those contortions willingly, and that's the witch's catch phrase. I saw the witch and Hanken lurking near the Capitol last week, dumpster diving for perks and she kept cackling that over and over."

"It looks like they're headed northeast." said Ned, looking through the field glasses. "The only place they could be headed is . . . no, don't tell me those two are behind this! Smore's taking her to The Cottage! They want Mary Jo? Why?"

"What is it about Mary Jo that would make her valuable to them?" queried President Washington. "Does she have special knowledge or skills? Would she be of value to someone else? Could she be traded for power or favor?"

"Power or favor . . . humm," said Ned thoughtfully. "Power or favor . . . I think I know why they want her!"

"Then tell me," Chad demanded, "what's this Cottage and who's behind it all?"

"Patience, sport, patience," cautioned Ned. "Wait for the rest of our raiding party. We'll see if the rest think my theory holds water, then we'll strategize, weaponize and mobilize!

Chapter 26
Poor, Poor Pitiful Smore

"Where are we going? That big baby has my bottle of kool-aid," Mary Jo yelled. "We have to go back and get it!"

"No can do, princess," said Mikhail. "We're on autopilot. That freak Sabine still has the phone. I can't do anything, so just sit back and enjoy the ride. We'll be there soon."

Mary Jo pouted and began looking through the garbage bags again. "If you won't tell me where we're going, I'll start throwing your stuff out," she threatened.

"You better not do that, sweetness," replied Mikhail. "Remember, I've got a lot of Barty's stuff in there too. He'd be really, really mad at you if you threw out anything that belonged to him."

Mary Jo continued going through the bags but didn't throw anything out.

"What's this?" she asked, holding up a tiny bottle.

"That's Barty's, just put that back, leave it alone," Mikhail said quickly. "He wouldn't want you to mess with that."

"I know what these bottles are used for," Mary Jo said coldly. "You mean Barty did this too?"

Mikhail sighed heavily. "Read his books, sweetness, read his books."

Mary Jo unscrewed the cap and tipped the contents of the bottle into her palm. The crystalline powder was bright blue. "It's kool-aid!" she exclaimed. "Quick – where's some water? Oh, kool-aid, kool-aid," she crooned. "It's been so long, quick, find the water, I NEED IT NOW!"

"The water's gone," said Mikhail. "We weren't supposed to be stuck up here . . . it was only supposed to be an hour or so . . . I didn't want to weigh down the sleigh . . ." he hurriedly tried to explain. "And that's not kool-aid, anyway, it's something else, it's experimental, it's BARTY'S! *DON'T TOUCH IT*!!!"

Mary Jo's nose delicately twitched at the powder in her palm. She smiled when she recognized the familiar scent. "You lie," she snarled at Mikhail. "It's kool-aid. You had it all along and you hid it from me. Barty won't mind if I have it."

Mary Jo lowered her face to her palm. She sniffed, snorted and snuffled the powder. When she raised her head, her mouth and nose were smeared a bright blue.

"AARRGGHH," she screamed, "I NEEDED THAT," and she passed out.

"No," stated Mikhail. "No. Absolutely not happening. This is just a dream. A nightmare!" Mikhail closed his eyes and pretended to sleep. He opened his eyes. "Hummm . . . still dreaming . . . oh, crap, this is no nightmare. This is just typical of my stupid, messed up life. I should have locked all that stuff up, I should have stashed it in Cuba . . . they'll say this is all my fault! Well, no way am I taking the blame for princess getting all stoked up on the Super Blue! Why'd *I* have the stuff anyway? Whose stupid idea was that? They should have known better! Yes! It's their fault – not mine. THEIRS!"

Mikhail scooted as far away from the comatose Mary Jo as was possible. "What's that stuff going to do to her?" he wondered. "It was bad enough when she smoked it and drank it out of the bong, but this . . . " Mikhail began to cry quietly. "I'm dead meat." He whimpered himself to sleep.

Chapter 27
And When She Awoke

"OW!" Mikhail yelled. "Please, no, princess, we're almost there. They've got *great* kool-aid, the *best*. I *promise*! Just hang on a little longer and . . . OW!" he screamed.

Mary Jo leaned out as far as she could, trying to reach Mikhail, who was swinging from the makeshift rope made from tied-together clothing. She had a Taser in her hand. She lunged and connected with Mikhail's forearm.

"EEEKKK!" he shrieked. "OW-OW-OW! Don't hurt me anymore, you evil little . . . OWWWWW!" he wailed as Mary Jo connected again. He began to twist and swing to avoid her. The ambulance sleigh rocked violently.

"Get down there!" Mary Jo ordered, "climb down that rope right now!"

"I can't," Mikhail sobbed. "I can't. I'm too scared!"

"HEY!" They heard a shout from below. "What's going on up there?"

"Now look what you've done," hissed Mary Jo. "You warned them. Now we can't sneak up on them. Act nice. Get us closer and you can jump on that baby. Take away his . . . MY bottle and throw it to me. Then you can kick that witch's butt, take back the phone and land this sleigh! Okay, there's the plan. Don't screw it up, you moron! Or else!" She jabbed the Taser in his direction.

"Sabine," Mikhail pleaded. "Help! She wants Hanken's bottle of kool-aid. Look! Look what she did to me! She's desperate. I swear to you, Sabine, she's really, really gotta have it. Please, toss Hankie's bottle up to her," Mikhail begged.

"Don't call him Hankie," sniffed Sabine. "I'm the only one who calls him that." She surveyed the situation and saw that Mary Jo did indeed look desperate, but no more so than Smore. The sleigh continued to rock.

"Okay," she said, "But only because we don't want those Cottage folks mad at us, do we Hankie?" she asked. "Give me that bottle."

"No," said Hal. "She's going to The Cottage. They've got *great* kool-aid – the *best! I'm* not going there, they don't invite *me*. This is all I have. The stupid twit is five minutes away from the good stuff."

"Hankie," Sabine pointed to the sleigh. "She's not gonna make it. She's going nuts. Remember what Mikhail said? We'd get invited to all the really important parties? Can't you give up one bottle for that?"

Hanken kept shaking his head.

"Hankie . . ." Sabine began, "you can be a hero. Look up there. They're going to tip and crash and burn. They'll all be killed. And do you know who those two in The Cottage will blame? Well, it won't be me. I tried to get her the kool-aid. I asked for the bottle. But did Hankie want to play nice? No, I'll have to explain that Hankie couldn't let go of the bottle, not even to save . . ." Hankie quickly handed over the bottle. ". . . his own ass," Sabine concluded. "Good boy, Hankie," she grimaced.

She whistled piercingly. "Heads up in the sleigh. Bombs away!" and she threw the bottle. It arced high in the sky, trailing a thin stream of blue liquid.

"No," screamed Mary Jo. "You're wasting it!" She jumped into the air and caught the bottle, immediately placing the nipple between her lips. "Aaahhh . . ." she sighed and settled into the passenger seat.

"Thanks, Sabine," called Mikhail, "thanks, Hankie . . . I mean Hal!"

Sabine scowled. "I still want a gun," she muttered. "He won't have that passenger on board forever."

Chapter 28
Welcome

"WTF?" said Mary Jo, peering into the distance. "Would you look at that? It looks like a huge bush of roses. Wait . . . is that a building under there? Is that The Cottage? Is that where we're going?" She pointed at the improbable sight set in the middle of a green valley.

"That's it, sweetness, that's The Cottage. It's covered with roses," Mikhail told her.

"D'oh!" Mary Jo scowled. "Do you think I'm stupid? Roses don't come in those colors. Not in lime, aqua, black, royal purple, peacock blue, brown, chartreuse, navy blue, tan, mint, baby blue . . . look at that forest green one!"

"There's rose colors too," Mikhail said. "Red, yellow, coral, fuchsia, orange, salmon, pink, ruby, white – look, real flower colors."

Mary Jo studied the roses as they got closer. "See!" she exclaimed, "I knew they couldn't be real. They're silk or something."

The sleigh landed. Mikhail fell out of it to the ground and began kissing it. "Thank you, thank you, thank you," he groveled.

Mary Jo opened the door and stepped out. She walked up to The Cottage and fingered the flowers. "Polyester," she sniffed disapprovingly.

The Cottage door opened. A woman stood in the doorway, dressed like a French maid. She was holding a plate of freshly baked cookies. "P-P-Pillory?" Mary Jo stammered, "is that you? What happened to you?"

"I lost the bet," Pillory said, opening the door wider. "Come on in. You look like you could use something to drink. Maybe some nice kool-aid?"

Mary Jo smiled and entered The Cottage.

Pillory got Mary Jo settled at the kitchen table with a glass of kool-aid and cookies. Lots and lots of cookies. There were oatmeal raisin, chocolate chip, ginger snaps, lemon bars, jumbles, hermits, sables and more. There were cookies on every surface. As Mary Jo nibbled a cookie and gulped her kool-aid, a buzzer rang and Pillory stopped stirring up more cookie dough long enough to take one sheet of cookies out of the oven and put in another.

"I'm sorry to hear you had some trouble getting here," said Pillory. "I knew Mikhail Smore would screw it up, but Will said . . . well, never mind about that right now. Have another cookie. Will will be here in a minute."

There was a laughing shriek in the hallway and Mary Jo turned to see Will, wearing boxers with cupids on them, black socks and an undershirt, chasing a scantily-clad Monique. "I'm gonna git you, you know I am, slow down, slow down there . . ." he panted. Monique complied and squealed as he grabbed her.

"Will!" yelled Pillory. "We have company."

"Okay, honeybunch, be right with you," called Will. "I just gotta get Monique here all comfy and cozy in my office. I'll be right down after that," he promised. "Oh, maybe twenty minutes or so, long enough for a good cigar."

Pillory sighed. "Oh, alright," she said. "Monique, don't you let Will fall asleep up there. And no more than *one* of those little blue pills. He eats them like candy if you don't watch him." She turned back to Mary Jo. "How about a kool-aid refill?"

"Sure," said Mary Jo. "This is *great* kool-aid! I *love* kool-aid! So what happened to you?" she asked. "I mean, you're old and all, and Will is too, so's that Monique person so it's not like I care or anything, don't get me wrong. I'm just curious. I mean, he's your husband, and he's chasing Monique around in your own Cottage . . . seems weird is all," she explained.

"Well, Mary Jo," said Pillory, "be careful what kind of bets you make. I lost a big one. I bet Will that I'd win the election. I agreed that if I lost, I'd live in a rose-covered cottage, dress like a French maid, bake cookies all the time and let him chase his floozies to his heart's content. So here I am," she explained. "Those roses on the cottage? Well, you might recognize some of my famous pantsuits!"

"Cool," said Mary Jo. "Those were pretty ugly."

"Why, you little twit," said Pillory angrily. "I tried to break the glass ceiling for you and women everywhere!"

"Huh?" asked Mary Jo.

Chapter 29
Who Are You?

"Who are these people?" Chad whispered to Ned, as dozens of ordinary looking people crowded into the room and helped themselves to the refreshments. Grandmas and grandpas, businesspeople, students, moms and dads, construction workers, police and firefighters, teachers, doctors and lawyers, dishwashers and waitresses, management and labor, farm workers and truck drivers – ordinary people you might see any day anywhere in the United States.

"Shhh," cautioned Ned. "The President is about to speak."

President Washington outlined the situation, then turned the briefing over to Ned. "Once again," Ned said, "thank you for coming. You know the infringements on our rights that we've already experienced and I know the country can count on you to step up and holler whenever our God-given freedoms are threatened." The audience applauded and Ned grinned. "Chad here asked who you are. I see my good friend Xo, I think I'll let him explain it."

Xo stepped to the front of the room. "Chad, I'm glad you asked that question. I'll tell you who we are. We are the most powerful force on earth. Our rights are granted by God and guaranteed by our Constitution. Life, liberty and pursuit of happiness are not just words to us, they are the fabric of our lives, they are woven into our hearts, our minds and our souls. We stand against tyranny and terrorism, even if the tyranny and terrorism is perpetrated against us by our own government! We do our due diligence, but we also practice due *vigilance*. You want to know who we are, Chad? I'll tell you who we are . . . WE THE PEOPLE, that's who we are!"

"WE THE PEOPLE!" agreed the crowd. "WE THE PEOPLE!"

Suddenly a male cheerleader dressed in red, white and blue cartwheeled into the room.

"Is that . . . ?" Chad wondered. "Couldn't be."

"Oh, yes it is," said Ned. "George W in the flesh." He chuckled as George W picked up a megaphone. "Watch this," he told Chad. "He really gets them fired up."

"Gimme a U!" George W yelled. The crowd complied.

"Gimme a S!" he continued. The crowd gave him an S.

"Gimme a A!" he screamed. The crowd did.

"What does that spell?" he asked the crowd.

"USA, USA, USA," they chanted.

"Who are you?" he asked.

"WE THE PEOPLE," they replied. The walls shook.

"I CAN'T HEAR YOU," he called.

"WE THE PEOPLE," they yelled. The ground rumbled.

"I STILL CAN'T HEAR YOU," he insisted.

"WE THE PEOPLE," they roared. Thunder boomed from the sky and the earth roared along with them. "WE THE PEOPLE, WE THE PEOPLE, *WE THE PEOPLE*!" They marched out of the room and boarded the waiting helicopters.

Ned and Chad climbed into a chopper. Xo was piloting it and there were five others in the back with an array of cell phones, signs and markers, laptops, fax machines, paper and pens, envelopes and stamps.

"You didn't mention why you thought they wanted Mary Jo," Chad said. "Did you decide you were wrong?"

"Not exactly," said Ned. "But GPS shows the sleigh is still near The Cottage. If we can get her there, before they move her or try to hand her off to someone else . . ."

"Someone else?" Chad asked. "Who?"

"Well, sport, I'm not entirely sure about that, but I do have my suspicions," muttered Ned.

"Did they grab her for Obantam?" asked Chad. "I still can't understand what the Flintons would want with her."

"Obantam doesn't care about your girlfriend," Xo told Chad. "He goes through those political virgins like grass through a goose. Besides, he's out of the country on another apology tour, and your girlfriend's been incommunicado since you crossed the border. He wouldn't even know she's gone off the grid."

"Xo's right," agreed Ned. "And the Flintons wouldn't be stupid enough to let her get hold of a phone or computer. The big cheese wouldn't care about losing a recruit, but with Smore and the Flintons involved it could get hairy if Mary Jo gets in touch with the outside world. The czars could be activated if Obantam felt threatened enough, and that would be a problem." Ned frowned.

Chapter 30
Hindsight is 20/20

"**I** still don't understand," said Chad, "how WE THE PEOPLE will rescue Mary Jo. I kind of expected the Founding Fathers . . ."

"Don't tell me," Ned said, "you expected the Founding Fathers to show up in superhero costumes, save Mary Jo, kick the bad guys out of office, right the wrongs and generally save the day." Ned and Xo both laughed.

"Well . . ." said Chad, "that would be nice. Where *are* the Founding Fathers?"

"Where are the Founding Fathers?" repeated Xo. "*Where are the Founding Fathers*? I'll tell you where the Founding Fathers are! They're all over the greatest country in history, the United States of America! They're in every state of the Union, in Ohio, Pennsylvania, Kansas, Texas, Georgia, Maryland, Alabama, Michigan, Florida, Colorado, Illinois, Indiana, Louisiana, North Carolina, West By God Virginia and everywhere patriots live across the nation. The spirit of the Founding Fathers lives on in the citizens who never protested anything before, but who went out and organized tea parties to protest runaway spending and government takeover. I was there, I saw it. I heard it. It lives on in the people who write to their elected officials and object to their actions – or their inaction, like voting 'present' 130 times. It lives on in the ones who show up at the town hall meetings and demand answers and accountability. The spirit of the Founding Fathers lives on in the watchdogs and whistleblowers and in all citizens who put country before party. No, Chad, the Founding Fathers aren't dead, they're very much alive."

"Then how did this mess happen?" asked Chad. "Why didn't the Founders see it coming and stop it?"

"They saw it coming, Chad, they did," Xo assured him. "They knew this could happen. Their writings warn over and over again about it. They worried that citizens would kick back and neglect to guard our freedoms. They worried that we would forget the lessons of history and find ourselves suffering under the yoke of oppressive government like they did. They set up a system of checks and balances to keep that from happening, but that's been hijacked."

"This shouldn't have happened, then," said Chad.

"No, it shouldn't have," agreed Xo. "But people forgot. They forgot how exceptional the U.S. is, and they even forgot the *meaning* of exceptionalism. They forgot how no people in earth's history had ever enjoyed the freedom that we did. They forgot to teach their children the history of our Founders and of this country and how to protect its freedoms. They lost rights bit by bit, gave up a little more power to government year by year. They allowed the schools to become indoctrination systems. They re-elected representatives who weren't really representing them, and they forgot about states' rights, allowing the federal government unprecedented control and intrusion into their lives. Then, to top it all off, they allowed the cult of personality to trump reason and common sense in the last election."

"Why didn't *we* see this coming?" asked Chad.

"Some did, and they tried to warn people," said Xo. "Mainstream media sold out and ridiculed and marginalized them. The media mounted all-out attacks on any conservative voice. Far left and foreign interests bankrolled and manipulated media in order to influence our election. Now many, many people are waking up and realizing that our country is being torn apart and forced into a direction that they don't want. They're realizing that campaign promises are just lies in disguise. The voters didn't vote for this kind of change, and they're mad as hell and not going to take it anymore."

"So now what?" Chad wanted to know. "How do we fix this?"

"Our Founding Fathers anticipated that we'd need a weapon," Xo told him. "They left us a powerful one – The Constitution of the United States of America, along with the Bill of Rights. The First Amendment guarantees us freedom of speech. All citizens need to exercise that right and voice their concerns to the government. Voting is another freedom of speech and should be exercised whenever possible, whether it's in local or national elections. If the people's representatives refuse to do the will of the people, vote them out and get someone in office who represents you. What's at stake here is nothing less than survival of the Republic itself. Let your voice be heard! Remember that the power is yours and use it. And if it gets really desperate, remember Article 5 of the Constitution and call for a limited Constitutional Convention to impose term limits on Congress and other federal employees, elected or not!" Xo smiled and winked. "And, of course, to repeal the 16th and 17th Amendments!"

Chapter 31
Don't Make Me Call The Secret Service

"Will," Pillory stood in the hallway and called up the stairs. "Will! Don't make me come up there!" Still no answer. She turned to Mary Jo. "Listen, I've got to go upstairs and get Will. He probably fell asleep. If the timer buzzes while I'm gone, take the cookies out of the oven. I don't want them to burn."

"Okay," Mary Jo agreed, munching on another cookie. Pillory went up the stairs, a plate of cookies in her hand. "Hummm," Mary Jo thought aloud. "I wonder where the TV is? I bet I'm all over the news. Chad's probably called out the Mounties by now." She continued to look around the room. "What's this?" she wondered as she moved a platter of cookies. "A laptop! Can't be theirs, the old fogeys wouldn't know what to do with it!" Mary Jo laughed meanly and fired up the laptop.

She heard Pillory's voice yelling above. "Will! Wake up! Monique! Get up and eat some of these cookies. Wait, Will, put your pants on first."

"Maybe I'll just check Alice's peagreenroom blog first. Check out what's happening with Cox & Hens," Mary Jo muttered. "I can't let the regulars think they ran me off. I'll call them names and insult them so much that *they'll* leave the blog!" Mary Jo bent to the keyboard and spewed her evil onto the blog. The buzzer sounded. Mary Jo ignored it and soon smoke was pouring out of the oven.

"What the . . ." Pillory exclaimed as she entered the kitchen. She turned off the buzzer, took out the pan of cookies, put it in the sink and ran water over the black, shriveled circles. "You didn't hear the buzzer, couldn't get the cookies out?"

"Well," sniffed Mary Jo, "I had more important things to do than listen for your buzzer or mess with your old cookies."

"Another Millennial that thinks they're too good for anything but an important position," snarled Pillory, "then turns out incompetent and is righteous about it!"

Mary Jo stuck her blue tongue out at Pillory – behind her back, of course.

"Will just stepped out to talk with Mikhail," said Pillory as she opened windows. She turned back to Mary Jo. "He'll be here in just a . . . what's that you've got? That laptop? No, that won't do." She held out her hand for the laptop. "That's Will's. No one's allowed to touch it. What were you doing? Emailing someone?" She continued to hold out her hand and snapped her fingers. "Don't make me call the Secret Service!"

"Okay, okay," said Mary Jo as she reluctantly handed over the laptop. "I was just blogging a little bit, don't get in a huff about it. I wasn't hurting Slicky Willy's precious laptop. I can't believe he uses this, since he's so old and not modern-thinking at all."

"Well, maybe you just don't know all that you think you do, missy," said Pillory, locking away the laptop. "Now have some more cookies while I check on Will and Mikhail. Sit!" She pointed at the chair. Mary Jo pouted her way to the chair and sat. Pillory left the room. Mary Jo heard voices. She listened hard, but couldn't make out what they were saying.

"Will," Pillory whispered, "she got hold of your laptop! She was blogging! You know what kind of trouble that's going to bring down on our heads? Where's that idiot, Smore? Did you settle up with him yet? He'll have to take her to . . ."

"Now, just settle down, honeybunch," said Will. "I've got the pills right here. I'll give Smore one for bringing her to us, and he can have the other if he agrees to deliver her for us."

"He's *got* to deliver her for us. That was the deal. He wasn't supposed to stop here at all!" Pillory was indignant. "Where'd you get those black pills anyway, Will?" she asked. "I thought they wouldn't even be manufactured until the new Deathcare Plan goes into effect."

"I have my ways," said Will. "Remember the two red pills Knute Ginger gave me years ago when the VRWC was after me and for awhile it looked like the only way out was to take the red pill? Well, I've been saving them for an emergency and I guess this qualifies."

Pillory looked into his palm. "Those pills are black, Will."

"Yep, a little food color fixed 'em up just fine," he replied. "And the best part is that Smore's never gonna know, because he won't be able to get Tweedledeedum and Tweedledeedumber to swallow the pills. Heads up their asses, you know!"

Will headed for the back door to talk to Smore while Pillory returned to the kitchen to get Mary Jo.

"NO, NO, *NO!*" yelled Mary Jo, clinging to the door jamb. "I won't get back in that ambulance with that freak! He's gross, he's disgusting, he's . . ."

"He's got kool-aid," Pillory interrupted her. "Don't make me call the Secret Service!" Mary Jo walked to the sleigh, her eyes on the baby bottle filled with bright blue liquid that Mikhail Smore waved at her.

Chapter 32
Who's In Charge Here?

"I can't believe I'm back in this stupid ambulance sleigh with big *old*, fat *old*, disgusting *old* you," she whined to Mikhail Smore.

"You think I'm happy about it, princess?" Mikhail said. "The boys and I," he said, pointing at his clones, Tweedledeedumb and Tweedledeedumber, "should have been back at the studio hours ago."

"Well, why'd you let Will and Pillory order you around? It's not like they're important anymore or anything," said Mary Jo.

"HA!" said Mikhail. "Just goes to show what you don't know. You never, never, never count those two out. *Never*. They're dangerous, they're sneaky and they know where a lot of political secrets are buried. They can twist your arm with a smile. Or they find out what you want, get it and use it as a bargaining chip." Mikhail patted his shirt pocket, where the black pills were hidden. He pulled out his cell phone.

"Hey," Mary Jo noticed, "you got your phone back!"

"Yes," said Mikhail. "The Secret Service got it from Sabine." He spoke into the clown's mouth and the sleigh rose into the air. Soon the rose-covered cottage was far below them. The sleigh flew to the northeast.

Mary Jo took a long pull at her bottle and sighed. "So where are we going now?" She began to kick at the back of Smore's seat.

"When are we going to get there? Are we going to meet Chad?" She kicked harder. "HEY!" she shouted. "Answer me!"

"Sweetness," Mikhail grinned meanly, "shut your trap. It's a whole new ballgame now that I've got my phone back. *I'm* in control, so forget about the yelling and kicking and screaming . . . OWWWW!" he shrieked as Mary Jo pulled his hair, bitch-slapped him and took away his phone, all at the same time.

"You're not in control of anything," Mary Jo told him. "And you're sure not the boss of me!" She began pushing buttons on the phone. "What's wrong with this stupid thing? I can't even call 911!"

"No-no-no," spluttered Mikhail. "You don't want to do that. Someone really, *really* important wants to meet you. I promise, we'll be there in an hour, hour and a half at the most. That phone's locked and it won't unlock until we get there. Besides, we're in Canada. No 911!"

"Really?" asked Mary Jo. "Why should I believe you? You said The Cottage people were important and wanted to meet me."

"They did!" exclaimed Mikhail. "They were glad to meet you! You'll see, they'll invite you to all the important parties now. They gave you cookies and the good kool-aid, didn't they? And now that you've met them, you're going to meet someone a lot more important than them. This is exciting!" Mikhail tried to cheer her up. "You hit the big time, sweetness! Now *you're* the important one, and they all want to meet *you*."

"Why?" asked Mary Jo. "Because Barty's going to leave that hag for me? That's a secret. No one knows that, except for you."

"Yes, that's it," Mikhail agreed quickly. "Because of Barty. You need to do just what Barty wants. He must have told a few important people about you, and they want to meet their future

Queen. Or it could be Empress. We'll just have to wait and see what titles Barty wants to use, right, princess?"

Mary Jo stared at him suspiciously. "Okay," she finally said, handing him the phone.

"That's better," Mikhail said. "Just relax, have some kool-aid, maybe take a nap. We'll be there before you know it."

Mary Jo settled back in her seat and sucked on the bottle of kool-aid. Soon her eyelids fluttered, the nipple slipped from her mouth and she slept. When she began to snore softly, Mikhail sprang into action.

"Let's just see who's the boss of you," he snarled under his breath while rooting through the garbage bags. "I know it's here somewhere. Ah ha!" Mikhail held up a straightjacket in triumph.

Chapter 33
Who's In Charge Now?

"OW, OW, OW!" Mikhail yelled as Mary Jo hit his head repeatedly with the straightjacket.

"HOW . . . DARE . . . YOU!" she shrieked, punctuating each word with a blow. "*Sweetness*, you called me, and *princess*! You said I'd be Queen or Empress, then you pull this crap! Barty will hear about this!"

"No, oh no," Mikhail babbled, trying to talk through slobber and snot. "It's not like that at all, princess . . ."

"DON'T CALL ME PRINCESS!" Mary Jo screamed. "You're a big, fat, ugly, disgusting LIAR!" Mary Jo kneed him in the groin and when he doubled over, she put the straightjacket over his head. She fastened it around his neck, crossed the sleeves in front of his chest and brought them up behind his arms, tying the ends at his Adam's apple. The only way for Mikhail to keep from strangling himself was to maintain a full-Nelson position.

"Nummf . . . pffst . . . mama . . ." Smore spluttered and huffed.

"You better shut up and sit down before you fall out," said Mary Jo meanly.

"Mmmm . . . ssss . . . uh . . . " Mikhail struggled desperately.

"What's that, moron?" asked Mary Jo. "Can't breathe? Not my problem!"

"Mummph . . . mummph . . . mummph . . ." Mikhail insisted.

"Oh, okay," Mary Jo said. "But I'm not letting you out of that thing. I guess I could cut an airhole . . . if I had a knife."

"Puh . . . puh . . . pahket!" Smore exclaimed.

"Eeeuuww," Mary Jo wrinkled her nose. "You'd like that, wouldn't you, you pervert? No way am I gonna reach into your filthy jeans!"

"Nuh . . . hug . . . sshurt!" Mikhail gyrated wildly as he tried to point to his shirt pocket with his chin and elbows and knees, almost strangling himself in the process.

Mary Jo patted his shirt pocket and felt the knife – and something else. She pulled the items out of Mikhail's pocket – the knife and two black pills. "What are these pills?" she asked Mikhail. "Something you were going to use on me?"

"Nuh . . . nug . . . mfff . . . mfff . . ." Mikhail whined.

"Oh, okay, you big baby," Mary Jo told him. She tucked the pills away under her skirt and flicked open the knife. "Hold still, this is going to be tricky. You better open your mouth so I can see where to cut." Mikhail's mouth opened under the material. Mary Jo hacked and sawed at the sturdy canvas with the little knife, finally cutting a slit over his mouth.

"AAAHHH," Mikhail breathed in deeply, then screamed it out the next second. "You freaking idiot! Are you nuts? You could have killed me!"

"Too bad your eyes are covered, you moron," she told him. "I bet you'd like to see me slice your clothes off. This knife is really sharp. Then I could start slicing off parts. What do you think, moron? Wouldn't you like to see that? How about I cut you some peepholes? You better stay real still, though. I don't want to get any nasty eyeball jelly on me and that could happen if you squirm."

Smore passed out.

"Good choice," said Mary Jo. "Now stay very, very still, and very very quiet," she told him as she went to work with the knife.

Mikhail remained passed out for a very long time, while Mary Jo got creative with the knife and other things from the garbage bags.

Chapter 34
Blog Pollution

"That's not Mary Jo," said Chad, peering below. "It's some crazy woman with her hair hacked off. She's all bloody, too. And she has a baby carriage with a huge baby in it!"

"Shoulda stapled that GPS to her butt instead of putting it in the Depends," muttered Ned, as he looked where Chad pointed. "That's Sabine and Hal Hanken down there. They must have the Depends. Gross!" Ned closed the laptop he'd been using to track Mary Jo.

"So all this time we've been following the wrong people? Mary Jo and that Smore creep could be anywhere! What do we do now?" Chad asked Ned.

Ned took off his hat and scratched his head. "Well, we could go to The Cottage and try to find out where they're going. Those two can keep a secret, though. We'd probably have to torture it out of them." He put his hat back on and unsheathed a hunting knife with an eight-inch blade. He tested the edge with his thumb and resheathed the knife. "Or we could go with my finely honed hunting instincts and anticipate where they're going . . ."

"Wait," said Chad. "I have an idea! Hand me that laptop. If Mary Jo did get online, she'd send me an email or tweet. I can't believe I didn't think of this sooner!"

Ned handed him the computer. "Don't get your hopes up, sport. Like I said before, Will and Pillory wouldn't let her get hold of outside communication."

Chad logged on. "No email or tweet," he said disappointed. "Maybe she checked in on that blog. She's real serious about that, she's always bashing Cox and the blog 'regulars'."

"We don't have much time, sport. Got to make a decision. So are you a gambling man, Chad?" Ned asked. "HA! Sure you are," he answered his own question. "Took a big gamble on your girlfriend, didn't you?" he chuckled. "So what's it gonna be? North to the border or play my hunch?"

"Your *hunch*? I thought it was your finely tuned hunting instincts," said Chad as he scrolled through the comments on the blog. "Hey! There she is – there's Mary Jo! That's her post!" Ned leaned over to read.

Comment by Mary Jo

"You're a bee-atch and a LIAR! I'm not paid by the healthcare industry to spread misinformation! I was never even political until the last eight years when the Republicans ruined the country!"

Chad kept scrolling. "Here's another," he said.

Comment by Mary Jo

"You don't know what you're talking about. Why don't you just crawl back into your hole, you moron! Cox isn't fair and balanced. You just follow their talking points. They're not even a news network, they're just entertainment!"

"And another," Chad said.

Comment by Mary Jo

"Hey, Moron-in-Ohio, get a clue! You're all just a bunch of racist idiots and you don't even know it. I'm leaving this blog and never coming back. I know I said that about 200 times before, but this time I really, really mean it!"

Chad kept scrolling as he and Ned read comment after comment.

Comment by Mary Jo

"I'm never going away. I'm queen of the blog and it's all about me because I'm so special! If I wasn't here, you'd all have nothing to talk about because you're all old and hateful and have no lives LMAO!"

Comment by Mary Jo

"My paper shows how you're all a bunch of racist idiots. You don't know anything. Do your DD! LOL LOL LOL! I might post it here and show you all how mean and stupid you are. Just don't hold your breath."

Comment by Mary Jo

"I'm sure you don't understand anything. That's what's shameful. Anyone with a brain would never vote Republican again or watch CoxNews, either, except if they're rich like Sannity and Heck and the other Cox jerks."

Comment by Mary Jo

"I'd like to know who you work for. Is it the Teabaggers? They SUCK! They are backed by a Republican Senator and big pharma. They are the real frauds, along with you regulars on this blog. Why don't you all go somewhere else?"

Chad and Ned looked at each other. "Well," said Chad, "you know, she gets really worked up over what people say on the blog."

"Worked up is one thing," said Ned, "but look what people commented to her. They didn't say anything extreme, but she just goes ballistic anyway. Look how she called the Tea Party patriots 'teabaggers' and called the regulars 'racist idiots' and 'frauds'! She's way 'round the bend, sport."

Chad stared at his shoes glumly.

"*HEY*!" Ned suddenly shouted. "Look at the time stamp – she's blogging right now! Blog back, sport, get her attention and find out where she is and what's happening!" Ned rubbed his hands together gleefully. "Oh boy, things are looking up, finally!"

Chad quickly began typing on the laptop.

Comment by Chad

"Mary Jo, where are you, I've been looking all over for you. I've been so worried!"

Chad hit 'submit' and waited impatiently. He didn't have long to wait.

Comment by Mary Jo

"Chat, WTF?! I got kidnapped by that fat moron in the Santa suit. Why didn't you rescue me? I'm still kidnapped! Where are you? You better do something RIGHT NOW! Get me out of here!"

Chad winced and replied.

Comment by Chad

"NOT ON A PUBLIC BLOG! Email me!"

He exited the blog and opened his email program to wait for Mary Jo's response.

Chapter 35
Chit Chat

Ding!

Chad received an IM from Mary Jo instead of the email he'd been expecting. "Darn," said Ned. "Well, that's okay, don't panic. You'll just have to shoot from the hip, get as much information from her as you can. Stall her about where you are, who you're with and what you're doing. Find out where she is!"

Mary Jo says:

"Chad, this is all your fault. This trip has been a nightmare and I just don't know if I want you for my boyfriend any-more. You let me get kidnapped by that freak show, I was bossed around and pushed around and he tried to put me in a straightjacket. You better get me out of this mess and I MEAN NOW!"

Chad and Ned looked at each other. "There's your 'out', sport," suggested Ned. "She's cutting you loose, doesn't want you for a boyfriend anymore."

Chad shook his head regretfully. "Nope. I can't do that. She's not in her right mind and I guess she hasn't been in a long time. If I don't take care of her and get her head straight, she'll just go on and on, attacking people on blogs and who knows what else. She won't just stop and go away. I'll deal with it. I appreciate all your help, Ned. I'll understand if you . . ."

"Nonsense," Ned said and slapped Chad on the back. "Toxic spill, aisle four! Clean up on the way! Right, folks?" he asked WE THE PEOPLE in the back.

There were sounds of agreement and encouragement from WE THE PEOPLE as Chad replied to Mary Jo.

Chad says:

"Really sorry, been following trying to get you back, ran into problems."

Mary Jo says:

"Problems? What problems? How bad could they be?" I'm the one who had problems!"

Chad froze. Ned thumped his back. "Car problems," he said. "Tell her you had car problems."

Chad says:

"Car problems, serious ones. Where are you, Mary Jo? I'll come get you right now!"

Mary Jo says:

"Where am I? How should I know? I'm not flying this thing, it's programmed or something."

Chad says:

"Is Smore still with you? Ask him."

Mary Jo says:

"He's here, but he's out of it. In shock or dead or something. Can't wake him."

Chad says:

"Are you headed north? Do you see any landmarks? Can you tell me what's on the ground?"

Mary Jo says:

"A bunch of freaking trees is what's on the ground! I can't see anything but trees! The compass says we're going northeast."

Chad says:

"Look around. Do you see anything else?"

Mary Jo says:

"Houses! With a big fence around them. Like a compound. Rich people!"

"I was right!" said Ned. "I knew they were trading her for something." He grabbed the field glasses and looked ahead. "There they are! We have to land when and where they do."

Chad sent a message to Mary Jo.

Chad says:

"We see you. We'll land when you do and pick you up. Just hang in there, Mary Jo, help is on the way."

He turned to Ned. "Now will you tell me where they're going? Who are they meeting and why do they want Mary Jo?"

"I think she's a gift for a party bigwig, sport," explained Ned. "Meant to pour oil, or kool-aid as the case may be, over troubled waters. To get on his good side. To heal a rift. To gain favor. To suck up."

Ned continued to track the sleigh through the field glasses. He suddenly lowered the glasses, shuddered violently, rubbed his eyes and shook his head. Chad reached for the glasses. "No," said Ned, holding them away from Chad. "Sorry, sport, but there's some things no one should have to see." Chad continued to reach for the glasses.

"Ned, she's *my* problem. I've *got* to see," Chad explained.

"Are you sure? I mean, once you see it, you can't *un-see* it," Ned told him.

"I'm sure," said Chad. Ned handed him the glasses and Chad raised them to his eyes.

Chapter 36
Red Rider Rides Again

Chad couldn't believe the sight that met his eyes. Up in the sky flew the ambulance sleigh. Mikhail Smore was standing between the driver's and front passenger's seats, tied in place with a rope made of torn and braided clothing. His jeans had been creatively cut into a close approximation of a thong and his legs were painted bright blue. Smiley faces adorned his butt cheeks. His bare chest had been powdered white and a big red M was painted n the center. ("What's this freak doing with all this makeup?" Mary Jo had wondered.) His hands were locked behind his neck and bands of canvas braced them in place. His head was covered tautly with canvas. The always artistic Mary Jo had gone to work with the knife, manicure scissors and the makeup to create a credible facsimile of a Mexican wrestler's mask. A blue dress bearing a copious white stain was tied at his neck and flew behind his as a cape.

Chad doubled over laughing and handed the field glasses back to Ned. Ned put the glasses to his eyes and took another look. He handed the glasses to Xo.

"Is she okay? What's wrong with her? Could she be having a stroke? A seizure? Does she have a history of . . . you know . . . mental illness? Is it that St. Vitus dance thing? Ants in her pants? Did her hands fall asleep?" Ned looked over at Chad, who was still laughing. "What the hell is wrong with her?!" he demanded. Xo began laughing too.

Chad fell to the floor of the chopper and laughed some more. He started to howl and hoot at the indignant look on Ned's face.

"Sorry . . . Ned . . . I . . . couldn't . . . help . . . it!" he panted. "The Masked Menace was a surprise, but I've seen the Jazz Baby before. Usually without any clothes on, though. Maybe Mary Jo's become a conservative!" he smiled hopefully.

"Don't go there, Chad. That's faulty reasoning." warned Xo. "Lots of liberals make the mistake of thinking that being conservative in politics means being conservative in all aspects of your life. It doesn't work that way, just like Mary Jo being conservative enough to keep her clothes on doesn't mean her politics have changed at all. You've been a closet conservative for a long time, Chad, come out and see the light. Remember the four basic principles of conservatism – respect for the Constitution, respect for life, smallest possible government and personal responsibility. How's your Jazz Baby stack up against those fundamentals?" asked Xo.

"Not too good at all," admitted Chad. "But . . . " he began.

"Now, don't get your dander up," Xo interrupted him. "We all know she got taken advantage of, she's higher than a kite on that junkie kool-aid and got hypnotized by Obigbad, but there's a wolf around every corner. Naïve political virgins get snapped up and eaten up every hour of every day, especially when a slick operator like that one is on the prowl. Look at her. She's out of control." Xo pointed at the sleigh.

Mary Jo had made some alterations to her outfit, shortening both her skirt and her shirt. She'd used makeup to whiten her face and hands and painted herself up as a mime. She'd used some of the clothes rope as a safety line to tie herself to the steering wheel as she danced on the hood of the ambulance. Her wild gyrations were punctuated by an abundance of 'jazz hands' as she grimaced and twisted, jumped and kicked. She started to shimmy and shake and began a very adult version of her 5th grade jazz recital number.

Chad sighed. "I just hope she'll be okay after the red pill," he said. "And if she is, I'll make sure she never gets near that kool-aid again," he vowed. "We'll read, study and learn about our Constitution and Founding Documents and our Founding Fathers' vision and plan for our country. We'll learn what we need to know to keep our freedoms. We'll watch our elected representatives and hold them accountable . . ."

"INCOMING!" Ned yelled.

Chapter 37
Look Into My Eyes

"It's the black helicopters," Chad yelled. "I didn't think they existed!"

"Oh, they exist, all right – too bad for us," Ned replied.

"There's so many of them," said Chad. "Forty-one, forty-two, forty-three . . . I can't count them, there's more of them all the time!" he exclaimed. "And look at that! Each black helicopter is wearing a white hat!"

"That's their feeble attempt to disguise their true evil intentions," Ned explained. "Lots of Americans grew up with movies and TV shows about cowboys. The white hats were the good guys and the black hats were the bad guys. Then the bad guys decided to change the rules and lie to people. They put on the white hats to make people think they were the good guys. When people questioned their actions, they'd point to their white hats and insist they were the good guys, all the while stealing them blind. By the time the folks woke up and realized their true intentions, the bad guys had stolen the ranch and the folks were working for room and board!"

"But who *are* they? And how did they get so much power?" Chad asked as he peered through the field glasses, first at the black helicopters, then at the sleigh. Mary Jo had stopped her wild dance and was standing at attention, saluting the black helicopters.

"They're the Czars, sport," explained Ned. "The top guy's personal shadow government, henchmen, cronies. They're his 'fixers', if something's not to his liking, he expects the Czars to fix it, with no oversight by Congress, which means no *interference* by Congress!"

All of a sudden a huge hologram projected by the Czars lit up the sky. The Salesman-in-Chief appeared, in glorious living color. The Twelve Teleprompters prepared to sing backup. They were dressed in a rainbow of choir robes.

"Oh, crap on a cracker," said Ned. "What's he trying to sell now?"

"Why are the Teleprompters dressed that way?" Chad asked.

"Okay, see that one in the red robe? That's WALNUT. The purple one is a union that backed Obantam – SCRU, I think. I can't remember what all the other colors represent. Hey, anyone got a chart for their color coding?" Ned called to WE THE PEOPLE. "Never mind, it doesn't matter. They're all special interest groups. Maybe foreign interests, for all we know."

"And he's the front man for them?" asked Chad.

"Have you ever been sold something you didn't want or need, or that wasn't good for you, but the salesman sold it to you anyway?" Ned asked Chad. "Ever been to a hypnotist or seen one on TV or in a Vegas show? That Vegas-style stuff, where they put people under in sixty seconds, is called 'black ops hypnosis'. Their secret's out and salesmen are using it too. How do you think he," pointing at the one hundred times life-size figure in the sky, "got to be Salesman-in-Chief?"

"So he uses these techniques to . . .?" Chad paused.

"First, to get elected!" Ned said. "Then to promote whatever the special interests direct him to through the Teleprompters. And punish or pay off anyone he can't snake charm. That's the Chicago Way. Now he's doing an end run around Congress with all these Czars, forming a shadow government and taking away the power that belongs to the people and is held in trust for us by our elected representatives. Looks a lot like the run up to a coup attempt, doesn't it, sport?"

"What . . ." Chad began.

"Look," Ned said. "Watch his hands. Look at those hand movements. Listen to the weird pauses when he's talking. See how his gestures work with the pauses? And his expressions? That's why he's so effective. He's practiced putting the entire package together and rehearsed his spiel. It's not so much what he says, which is mainly feel-good BS anyhow, but *how* he says it. If you don't know what he's doing, you get a warm, fuzzy feeling and want to buy the BS and please him by doing what he wants! Don't worry, now that you know what he's doing, you're immune to it."

"What can we do to get our power back?" Chad asked.

"Watch this," Ned told him. "Ready back there?" he called to WE THE PEOPLE.

"READY!" they roared.

Chapter 38
The PEOPLE Speak

"**O**kay," Ned transmitted through the radio to the other choppers, also carrying WE THE PEOPLE. "Light them up!"

"Light what up?" Chad asked. "I don't see any lights."

"Of course you can't see them, sport. Patriot rays are invisible," Ned told him. "See what looks like searchlights on the choppers? Watch what happens when they aim those at the Czars."

Chad looked at Heck's chopper, which had a huge searchlight. He watched as Heck aimed it at the Czars. Sure enough, as soon as the invisible rays found the Czars, hundreds, maybe thousands, of lines of thin blue light became visible. WE THE PEOPLE immediately began writing, emailing, phoning and faxing.

"I don't understand this at all," said Chad. "What's going on?"

"Those blue lines are the Czars' connections," Ned explained. "They can try to keep them hidden, try to keep them secret, but they're no match for Heck, Big Rushbo, Sannity and the rest."

"What are the connected to?" Chad wanted to know.

"They're connected to special interests, past speeches and published works, foreign interests, social engineering, dubious associations, eugenics, deathcare proposals, unions, big money and a whole lot of -isms that Americans don't like – stuff like Communism, Socialism, Fascism," said Ned. "They're really bad news for America. They don't report to anyone but the guy that brought 'em to the dance." Ned jerked his chin at the figure in the sky. "See how they've all got blue lines to him? And there's more lines that connect to his administration and others in government."

"Isn't that un-Constitutional?" Chad asked.

"Nope," Ned replied. "He can have 'assistants', but did you ever know any President to need as many assistants as that one? And at what cost to the taxpayers? His wife has a whole slew of assistants, too, costs the taxpayers over $1 million a year for them."

"So Congress doesn't oversee any of this?" Chad was upset.

"Nope again," Ned said. "He's busy transferring power from Congress. Sometimes they don't know it until it's too late because they're voting on the bills without even reading them. It's all done in a big, crisis-type hurry. The bills are too complicated and there's too much hidden in them. Not to mention that the bills themselves are written by special interest groups! Congress isn't doing its job anymore, and so our system of checks and balances is out of whack."

There was a flurry of activity in the rear of the chopper. WE THE PEOPLE were furiously writing, emailing, phoning and faxing their Congresspeople about the ominous connections to the Czars that had been exposed by the searchlights. They demanded that power be restored to WE THE PEOPLE, or to their duly elected representatives. They demanded clearness, transparency and accountability. They strongly objected to how the United States was being changed. They insisted that Congress stop the runaway spending, slow down, read the bills and stand for the people.

Suddenly the thieving badgers appeared below. Soon various members of the pack would start to vibrate, then they'd fly into the air, as if launched from a catapult, aimed directly at the Czars. When they hit the Czars, many clung like leeches and would not let go. Others fell back to the ground.

"My God," said Chad, shocked. "They're like that killer rabbit from the Monty Python movie! Why are they doing that?"

"When Heck and the others manning the searchlights expose the connections and dirty secrets, WE THE PEOPLE go into action by exercising their freedom of speech to make their voices heard. When a thieving badger gets enough of these complaints, its fear of losing votes activates its survival sense and it goes into attack mode," Ned explained.

"I see," said Chad. "But some seem more serious than others."

"The ones that fall back are the fence-sitters, the moderates, the progressives, the elites who think they know better than the people who put them in office. They make a half-hearted attempt, pay lip service and then do just what they were doing before. Then they're hit with more letters and calls until that survival sense kicks in again and they attack again," said Ted.

"But how will this get rid of the Czars?" Chad asked.

"When enough of them," Ned pointed at the thieving badgers, "get enough complaints and objections from WE THE PEOPLE, the attacks will overwhelm and take down some of the Czars and some connections. If the thieving badgers aren't motivated enough to stand for the people, WE THE PEOPLE will vote them out next election cycle and get someone in who actually does represent the people. Remember what Thomas Jefferson said, *'When the people fear government, it's tyranny, when government fears the people, it's Liberty'.*"

"Hey, Chad," Xo called. "There goes your girlfriend!"

Chad looked where Xo pointed and saw the sleigh coming in for a landing in the center of the compound below where a bizarre tableau awaited Mary Jo's arrival.

Chapter 39
A Goat By Any Other Name

Mary Jo stepped out of the sleigh and looked around. She'd landed in a large grassy area where the creatures now circling her had been playing football.

"Wow!" she exclaimed. "I thought you were guys on horses. Playing like, you know, Pogo. Then I thought you were those half man, half horse things. But no. So you're what, part goat and part man? What do you call that?"

"Satyrs," the ring of satyrs chorused. Their hooves shuffled restlessly as they edged closer to Mary Jo.

"And you play football. I wouldn't think goats were smart enough for that." Mary Jo looked around for the goats' owner.

"Satyrs," the satyrs chorused, and moved closer still.

"Phew!" exclaimed Mary Jo. "Back off some, would you? You goats are really stinky, aren't you?"

"Satyrs," the satyrs chorused, and closed in.

"So you don't know anyone important around here, huh?" she asked. The satyrs pressed up against her.

The smell woke Mikhail Smore. "Whew!" Mikhail shook his head, then noticed what was going on. "HEY! You satyrs get away from her! Don't you know who this is?" he asked. "This . . .," he paused for effect, ". . . is *Mary Jo!*"

The satyrs backed away. "Mary Jo . . .?" they muttered.

"M-M-Mary Jo," stuttered a randy old satyr with a full mane of white hair who'd been watching the football game from the sidelines. With difficulty, being a corpulent satyr, he got off his haunches and moved slowly toward the others. "Mary Jo," he bleated beseechingly, his arms outstretched. "My Mary Jo! You came back to me!" his suddenly stentorial voice boomed. He pointed a trembling finger at the group of satyrs. "She's mine! All mine! You can't have her! I waited forty years for her!" He began to snort and paw the ground, preparing to fight or rutt or both.

"*NO!*" screeched Mary Jo. "You stay away from me, you horny old goat!" ("Satyr", the satyrs chorused.) She scrambled back into the sleigh and began to cut the straightjacket binding Mikhail Smore's arms. "You get me out of here right now, you moron," she told him. "You took me to the wrong place. He," she pointed to the Salesman in the sky, "is gonna be really, *really* pissed at you!"

Smore moaned and rubbed his arms, then ripped off the blue dress cape and straightjacket mask. "Calm down, sweetness, I'll take care of everything. Where's your kool-aid?" he asked.

"I ran out," Mary Jo sulked. "They didn't pack enough."

"How could you run out," Mikhail began angrily, then stopped himself. "Well, never mind, it's all good. I'm sure the goats . . . er, satyrs," he corrected at the look the satyrs gave him, "have some kool-aid. They'll fix you right up, soon you'll be feeling great! Just go along up to the house with them, you'll be fine."

"Mine! My Mary Jo," the horny old satyr snorted, pawing up a patch of turf. He opened his palm and displayed two little, light blue pills – not the kind that was in the kool-aid. He swallowed them. "MINE!" he bellowed.

"Are you out of your freaking mind?" Mary Jo asked Smore. "Look at them! That's not the finger they're flipping me! Look at that disgusting horny old one! I know what those little blue pills are! Now *GET ME OUT OF HERE*" she screamed.

"Look," Mikhail pointed behind her. "Is that some kool-aid?" Mary Jo turned to look.

"Where . . ." Mary Jo began. She was cut off by Mikhail, who thunked her on the head with the surprisingly heavy cell phone. Mary Jo slumped onto the seat. Mikhail began to tie her up with the rope of braided clothing. He glanced at the threatening figure in the sky. Suddenly it began to spark and fizzle. Sections began to fade away.

"Ed," he called to the horny old satyr, "this Mary Jo is a GIFT, a PRESENT for you. You know, for the anniversary. She's from WILL and PILLORY. Remember that – a *PRESENT* from *WILL* and *PILLORY*. They're really, *really* sorry that they backed the peanut farmer back when instead of giving you their support. They understand that you were really hurt by their actions, so you backed the Salesman instead of Pillory. They hope this gift, this Mary Jo, will heal the rift and seal the deal. When the Salesman crashes and burns, they want your support. So, big guy – is it a deal?" Mikhail finished tying up Mary Jo, who was beginning to come to.

"Yes, yes, yessss, we have a deal. They'll have my support. Now give me my present. *GIVE ME MY MARY JO!*" he demanded, drooling over the name. He snorted and pawed the ground furiously. The effect of the little blue pills was obvious.

"Okay, okay," said Mikhail. "Just wait a minute while I check something." He patted his shirt pocket and discovered he had no shirt. He checked what was left of his jeans, but the pockets were gone. "Why, you little . . . " he began, shaking Mary Jo awake, "what did you do with my pills?"

"Pills?" Mary Jo mumbled groggily. "What pills?" She noticed she was tied up and began to struggle. "You freak! You were going to give me to those horny goats!" she accused him.

"Satyrs," the satyrs chorused.

"MINE!" thundered Ed. "*I WANT MY MARY JO!*" His hooves shredded the grass and pawed up dust.

"Wait!" Mikhail ordered. "I have to have those pills! They were my payment for delivering her!" He began burrowing through the contents of the sleigh. He paused to snarl at Mary Jo. "Those are *my* pills and I want them *NOW*!" He reached out to shake her again and was astonished to see that her hands were free and she was holding the Taser.

"*D'OH!*" Mary Jo exclaimed. "It's your own fault, you stupid moron! I told you not to use the stretchy clothes when you braided that rope." She threatened him with the Taser. "Now pick up that phone and *GET ME OUT OF HERE!*" she demanded.

Chapter 40
Missed Her By *This* Much

The battle raged on as Chad and Ted's chopper swooped down to rescue Mary Jo. The huge image of the Salesman in the sky shimmered and shook. The heavy bombardment was ripping away his disguise and exposing his true nature as the Czars' power was challenged. Soon the image revealed a shirtless 'leader of the free world', wearing mom jeans and showing off his snake-oiled man boobs. His patented expression of arrogance, contempt and superiority was on full view. A sideways ball cap bearing the words 'It's America's Fault' and a cigarette dangling from his lips completed the picture. In the background, the Twelve Teleprompters were fighting, hurling insults at each other just as fast as they could scroll.

"Will they be okay?" Chad asked as he looked back at the helicopters carrying WE THE PEOPLE.

"They'll be fine. Remember, this is just a battle, not the whole enchilada. We may lose a skirmish or two, but you can be sure we're going to win the war," said Ned. "Look!" Ned pointed to a black ops/white hat helicopter, corkscrewing out of control and belching fire and smoke. "WE THE PEOPLE just shot down that Czar!"

"Oh no," said Chad, his attention once again on the ground. "It looks like Mary Jo is in trouble. Those goats are trying to molest her! We have to hurry!"

"My fault, sport. Meant to be there when she landed, snatch her up before those horny goats could get to her. Actually, they're not goats, they're satyrs," Ned told him, and quickly explained the history of the feud between Ed, Will and Pillory.

"Why, those . . ." Chad was incensed. "That's human trafficking, that's despicable. Trading her off to be used for a sex toy! How low can they go?"

"Trust me, sport you *do not* want to know. But everyone *needs* to know. Too many politicians think that 'the end justifies the means' and 'some are more equal than others', so they feel that the rules and laws don't apply to them because they're so special.. In case you haven't noticed, America has an aristocracy – politicians! They live large on the taxpayer dollar while telling the rest of us to cut back. They attack American citizens who are exercising their right of free speech, calling them 'evil-mongers', 'Astroturf', 'teabaggers', 'fringers', 'un-American' and more while they write laws that apply to us and not to them. They are trying to shut down any opposition, including the Constitution, trying to take away our rights, and all the while they tell us it's for our own good." Ned ranted. "They think they know how to run our lives better than we do. They're arrogant elitists who see the rest of us as stupid sheeple who have to be told what to do. Well, they're getting a wake-up call now!"

"What the . . ." Ned began, once again looking through the field glasses at the sleigh. "They're taking off! No, wait, they're coming back around. What are they trying to do? They're buzzing the goats! Are they trying to run them down?"

Ned turned to Chad. "She's holding a Taser on Smore! She's making him buzz the compound and run down the goats." Ned looked at the scene below and suddenly started to laugh. "Ha!

Look, the goats are bringing kool-aid packets and throwing them at the sleigh. I guess she ran dry."

"Let me see," said Chad. Ned passed the glasses to him. He watched as Mary Jo ripped open a packet of kool-aid and poured the powder into her mouth. She jabbed the Taser at Smore as he spoke into his phone's clown mouth and gave the clones instructions. The sleigh shot into the sky and headed north. "What do we do now?" asked Chad.

"We follow," Ned answered. "Fire up that laptop. See if you can reach that crazy . . ." Ned stopped. "Sorry, sport. We'll get her back. Go ahead and try to contact her."

The helicopter followed the sleigh north as Chad used the laptop to try to reach Mary Jo.

Chapter 41
Time to Regroup

The sleigh flew north, heading for the Alaska border. The helicopter followed.

"I can't get a connection," Chad complained. "What kind of service do they have up here? What do we do now?"

Ned used the field glasses to watch the occupants of the sleigh. "They're fighting," he told Chad. "She's winning." He appeared thoughtful. "We need a new strategy." He frowned, then suddenly cheered up. "I've got it!" he exclaimed. He dug through a rucksack and produced a device that looked like a futuristic ray gun and aimed it at the sleigh.

"*WAIT!*" yelled Chad. "Don't vaporize them!"

"Relax, sport, Ronny here won't vaporize anyone. Not until I push this button here, anyway," Ned corrected himself. "Right now old Ronny Ray-Gun is in jamming mode. Let's just see if we can mess with their communications system" Ned aimed the gun again and bright red, white and blue rays shot towards the sleigh. Ned had hit them with the rays while they were making a left turn, so they were stuck circling in the air while Mikhail Smore furiously shook the non-responsive phone and Mary Jo threatened him with the Taser. "That should hold them for at least an hour." He gave the pilot a new heading. "Lucky for us we're so close," he said. "We'll be there in five minutes."

The helicopter flew on while Chad watched the circling sleigh until it was out of sight. He turned his attention to the ground when the helicopter began to descend.

"HEY!" he shouted. "That's a *LAKE* down there! I don't remember seeing pontoons on this chopper! Aren't we too close to that cliff?"

"No worries, Chad," Ned told him. "Remember the smoke and mirrors you saw the left-wing loons using? Well, these good folks use pixels." The helicopter gently settled on the surface of the lake. Chad and Ned deplaned. The 'lake' felt like concrete and wasn't wet at all.

"HALT!" called out a long-haired, mustachioed figure wearing mountain man garb, as he stepped out of a hut nestled beside the cliff. "Who goes there?!" he demanded, pointing a long rifle at them.

"Whoa, Dog, it's me, Ned, and a friend, name of Chad Sixpack." Ned swirled his finger above his head and motioned the chopper to take off. "Chad, this is my good friend, DogOnCrack. Don't let the name fool you, he doesn't do any crack. He's not really a dog, either. He's just a hardcore, right-wing, devout Christian, conservative libertarian who is hellbent on liberty and justice!" Ned laughed as he recited Dog's well-known self description.

DogOnCrack studied Chad through narrowed eyes. "Sixpack, you say? Come on in. There's some folks who'd be really interested in meeting you."

"Me?" asked Chad. "Come in where?" He pointed to the hut.

Dog nodded and motioned them into the hut. He tapped a few commands into a computer and the shack disappeared, replaced by a beautifully appointed foyer. A long hallway was at the foyer's end. Chad turned to look behind and saw that the lake was now a landing pad and the cliff had disappeared and been replaced by a huge inverted glass bowl.

"Bio-Dome!" Chad gasped.

"No," replied DogOnCrack, "it's Bunker II." He turned and walked down the hallway. Chad and Ned followed.

Chapter 42
Meet and Greet

Chad grabbed Ned's elbow and whispered urgently. "The *bunker*? I think I might know these people. Mary Jo blogs with a bunch of crazies that have a bunker. She says they're all right-wing extremists and . . ."

"Hey, sport," Ned cut him off, "think it through. These folks aren't dangerous. They didn't get your girlfriend hooked on the kool-aid. They didn't try to trade her off to a horny old goat. If you check the blog archives, you'll see that all they did was to try to get her to educate herself, open her eyes and learn from history. They're not the ones off in Shangri-La-La Land, drugged on kool-aid."

Chad bowed his head and rubbed his eyes. "Sorry," he muttered. "I guess I'm not thinking straight."

"Well, you've been lied to, sport," Ned said, "by someone you trusted. Hard to get over that, but a dose of reality should help. And if that doesn't work, there's always a swifte kick in the pants!"

Dog was waiting for them by a set of double doors. He'd secured his gun in a rack and shucked off his buckskin tunic to reveal a Reagan tee-shirt. He waggled his eyebrows at Chad.

"Please, step into our parlor," he invited. "Enter the lair. The Coliseum and the lions are right this way." He grinned wolfishly, opened the doors and motioned them in with a sweeping gesture.

"INCOMING!" DogOnCrack announced them.

"Now, Dog," chastised a smiling woman dressed in bright colors. "We don't announce guests that way." She laughed and the ice in the pitcher she held seemed to laugh with her. "Anyone care to join me in a Bunkertini?" she asked. "I just mixed up a batch. Have a seat, make yourselves comfortable. I'll be back in a flash with the glasses." She left the room so quickly she seemed to disappear.

"Sit," said Dog. He lounged on a curvy couch and strummed a guitar that displayed a 'Peyton' sticker. Chad and Ned joined him. Dog handed Ned another guitar and the two strummed companionably as Chad looked around.

The room was huge, but cozy with groupings of furniture here and there. Plenty of computers were in sight, as well as many musical instruments, books and magazines, paintings and photos. There was an indoor lagoon complete with beach sand and tropical foliage and fire pits. Chad looked up and saw the night sky filled with stars and a magnificent full moon. There seemed to be no ceiling to the room. A balmy, ocean-scented breeze completed the tranquil atmosphere.

The woman returned, carrying a tray with glasses and snacks. She poured the Bunkertinis and passed the glasses around. She took a seat opposite Chad. "Cheers!" she said, taking a sip of her Bunkertini. "Yum! That hits the spot." She smiled at Chad. "Try it, you'll like it," she encouraged him. "Or I can get you something else, we've got just about everything you could imagine here. Everything except kool-aid, that is!"

Chad tasted the Bunkertini. "This is great," he said. "I don't mean just the drink, either. This place – it's amazing! I never thought a bunker could look like this." Chad took another sip of his drink. "I'm sorry," he said. "I didn't catch your name."

"Just call me Cookie," she replied. "Would you mind if I asked a personal question? Are you wearing one of those shaper thingys? You know, the man-girdle with fake abs?"

"No," Chad answered, "why would you ask? That seems like an odd question."

"Hummm," she said, "just curious. Actually, it was something your girlfriend said on the blog."

"I''m sorry," Chad said quickly. "Mary Jo hasn't been herself lately. It's the kool-aid . . ."

"Now, Chad, we all know it's not just the kool-aid," she chastised him. "She's been indoctrinated by liberal schooling. She's stayed in school, an artificial environment, instead of getting out in the real world. She's never been taught to listen, think and discern. She's been fed a diet of revisionist history and outright lies by ultra-left professors. She's a mess, Chad!"

Chad sighed. "I hope this red pill thing works out," he said. "If it doesn't . . . well, I don't know what I'll do."

"My point is that she'll need lots of work even after the red pill," said Cookie. "And much of it is work that she'll have to do on her own, such as reading some *real* history as well as our Founding Documents. She needs to know how the Progressives, the far-left and foreign interests have peddled poison to American citizens. She needs to see government's *real* role in our country's history and realize how they've betrayed the citizens by abandoning the Constitution. It won't be easy, Chad," she told him.

"That's okay," said Chad. "I'll help her. I *want* to help her. I need to learn too. We'll study, we'll learn, we'll do better. We'll be careful with our votes and not toss them like candy to a flashy salesman hawking pie in the sky." Everyone's gaze was drawn to the night sky by Chad's pointing finger.

"Yikes!" exclaimed Cookie, as the ambulance sleigh flew across the full moon in a weird parody of a Halloween witch.

"Trick or Treat," said Dog.

A muted chime sounded. Cookie picked up a remote, pushed a button and a giant monitor appeared on a wall.

"Here she is now," Cookie told him, as Alice's peagreenroom blog appeared on the monitor. "It seems she's got a lot to say, as usual." She grimaced. "Too bad practically all of it is either incorrect or pure vitriol, or both!"

Chapter 43
Rant On

Mary Jo blogged, and her words appeared on the monitor.

"You're all old and stupid. You can't even understand that it's all Bush's fault! Everything was fine until the last eight years! Bush trashed the economy – what don't you understand about that? He spent all that money on the war, now we have to spend more to fix it."

Chad watched as others on the blog tried to educate Mary Jo, to no avail. Facts and figures were presented, but Mary Jo ignored them all. She exhibited a tour de force of bad behavior: rudeness, disrespect, name calling and ridicule of other bloggers, CoxNews, Cox and Hens, and the blog's hostess, Alice. Chad squirmed uncomfortably and his face flushed as Mary Jo went on and on, sounding more and more ridiculous and out-of-control with each comment she made.

Comment by Mary Jo:

"Everyone knows these people were incited by Republican-controlled websites and other Astroturf groups who made insurance company employees attend townhalls and shout down the representatives. They will stop at nothing, and that means brainwashing ignorant people who don't under-stand what the change will do to them."

Comment by Mary Jo:

"I meant for them, not to them, you morons should know that. The past administration were the big spenders, not this one! The second, I mean the first, stimulus is only 10% spent so far! Do you really understand how that works? I don't think you do. It worked great in China. If you understand, explain it to me here so I know that you really do get it. I don't like just getting what everyone hears on CoxNews, because we all know how biased that opinion is!"

Comment by Mary Jo:

"Why don't you morons watch another news channel and see what's really going on? ASMBC anchors are a lot more informed than Cox anchors. Cox is just entertainment, ASMBC has the real news! This blog is useless. Alice ought to just shut it down. Cox isn't relevant, anyway. I don't know how they can call themselves a news outlet. The world would be better off without this blog and CoxNews!"

"Yikes!" exclaimed Cookie, "I think we've had enough of that for awhile," she said as she switched blogs. Suddenly a group of people appeared in the room. Some were holograms, some were on monitors. One remote hook-up seemed to come from the back of a turnip truck. Cookie made introductions, and Chad realized that these were some of the people Mary Jo had been attacking on the blog.

"I don't understand," said Chad. "Do you all live here in Canada?"

"No," Cookie said, "and you're not in Canada anymore, Chad. Bunker II is built on good old U. S. of A. soil, right here in the great state of Alaska! Some of the people you see are in their own homes, some are at our original Bunker – 'Home Free', it's called. The turnip truck is right here at Bunker II. At least it is for now – that truck does seem to travel around a lot!" she laughed.

"You all seem like really nice people," Chad began, "and I'm really, really sorry . . ."

"We don't want apologies, Chad," Cookie cut him off. "What we want now is information." She leaned forward and stared into Chad's eyes. "What's her agenda? Who's she working for?" She continued to stare at Chad. "I know you know," she told him. "Spill it!"

"Well, uh, uh . . ." Chad stammered. "Okay, I do know what her agenda is, and now I know how wrong it is too. She's determined to shut down the peagreenroom blog. That's her assignment, and she got it right from the top, I think. Her "Uncle" – you know who I mean." He glanced around nervously.

"Hummmm," said Cookie, "that's what we figured. The kool-aid Salesman himself! I bet he'd love to silence CoxNews and silencing the voices on the blog would be a good start. His buddies in mainstream media are losing viewers by the thousands and want him to eliminate the competition. This is an attack on not just a media outlet, but on free speech itself!"

The others murmured agreement, but appeared worried.

"Oh, relax," Cookie said cheerfully. "Cox won't roll over and close a blog just because its been infected by a radical rat. Can you imagine the outcry from their viewers? I bet Cox is investigating this blog invasion. It would be a big story if she were a plant from another news outlet, but if the plant is from the Salesman, or his party . . . that's *huge*. Nope, it wouldn't surprise me one little bit if Cox was already all over this one."

"Oh, no," Chad moaned, dropping his head into his hands. "This just keeps getting worse and worse! Investigated by Cox! Well, I guess she's in a conspiracy, all right. How did all this happen? I just wanted a nice, quiet life, not this mess." He looked at Cookie beseechingly. "If I can grab Mary Jo, get her away from Smore, can we just stay here? I promise . . ."

"*NO!*" The bunker group yelled as one.

"I know what you wanted, Chad," Cookie told him. "You wanted a 'nice quiet life'. You wanted to remain a closet conservative so you could go along to get along. You didn't want to stand up for your convictions because you didn't want to be called 'racist', 'hate-monger', 'evil' or 'anti-American' by community organizers, the far left and mainstream media. That's what they were counting on. Mary Jo isn't the only one who refuses to be swayed by facts. How many warning signals did you get about past associations and actions, the 'Chicago Way' and even actual audio and video recordings of what the Salesman planned to do to this country? No, you had plenty of warnings and ignored them. You, along with millions of others, have been and are being manipulated and intimidated. Educate yourself, Chad. The truth will set you free. Read Saul Alinsky's 'Rules For Radicals' and see how the far left is using it to take this country in a direction the majority of its citizens don't agree with. Wake up, stand up and help America get back on the right path!"

The bunker group voiced their agreement while Ned and Dog began playing 'The Star-Spangled Banner' on their guitars.

Chapter 44
Under My Bus

Mary Jo blogged her little blue kool-aid heart out while Mikhail Smore desperately searched through the garbage bags for a phone charger.

"It was here, you little twit, right here!" said Mikhail, exasperated. "You threw it out, I know you did. So now we're stuck flying in circles, and it's making me sick." With that, he leaned over the side and puked again.

"Shut up, shut up, shut up," Mary Jo muttered. "Can't you see I'm busy? I'm educating these stupid people on this blog. Someone has to correct all their misinformation and I'm not stopping until they all wise up, drop dead or go away!" She typed furiously. "Or until we shut down this blog or CoxNews, whichever comes first," she amended.

"You won't be so calm about this when the kool-aid wears off and you need another fix," said Mikhail.

"What do you mean?" asked Mary Jo. "Those goats were throwing dozens of packets. I even caught one! Where are the rest?" She looked around the sleigh, then glared at Smore accusingly. "You threw them out!" she snapped. "You mean, vicious, fat, old moron!"

"You little fool!" he exclaimed. "Those goats just wanted to get rid of us. They weren't giving up their kool-aid supply for you or anyone else. You're just lucky they didn't toss you the Jim

Jones brand kool-aid!" He turned away and mumbled something about a missed opportunity.

"What?" Mary Jo's voice lowered menacingly. "You mean there's no kool-aid?" She tossed him the laptop. "Contact someone! Email them, tweet, IM, whatever – *JUST GET ME SOME KOOL-AID!*," she shrieked. "Get Barty! He'll come and get me and you'll wind up in prison – or worse!"

"Barty? Get *Barty*? HA! That's a good one," he chuckled. "Haven't you been paying attention, sweetness? You're – *we're* a liability to Barty. And what does Barty do with liabilities? He throws them UNDER THE BUS! Yep, Grandma, Bill Scares, Reverend Rightnow, Mezko, Shaklidi, Auntie. Where are they now? All thrown under the bus just as soon as they become a problem. Used and tossed under the bus. Thrown away and run over." Smore looked at Mary Jo sadly. "That's where we're headed, princess. Under the bus. All we have to do is try to contact Barty . . ."

"Nonsense," said Mary Jo firmly, and took back the laptop. "I'll contact him. Everything will be okay, you'll see. I'm not a liability. You," she sniffed, "you're the liability."

"WAIT!" Mikhail yelled, and spread his hand over the keyboard. "You're right, I'm a liability. I got in his way, I screwed up his plan, I cut a deal with his enemies, and I already made that fake healthcare documentary, so I'm no more use to him. But *you*," he continued, "you've been all hopped up on the kool-aid and you've been seen with his enemies. Kool-aid withdrawal makes you a loose cannon and that makes *you* a liability. He knows that his enemies can buy you with a packet of kool-aid." Mary Jo slapped his hand away.

"NO," she screamed. "You're not stopping me! I'm getting Barty right now!"

"I won't stop you," Mikhail said, resigned to his fate. "Go ahead, call Barty." He sighed and shuddered. "Just one favor first, princess. After all we've been through, show a little mercy to a doomed man and give me those black pills . . . please," he pleaded.

"Pills? Black pills?" Mary Jo mused. "Okay, I'll give you those pills. Now where did I put them?" She tapped furiously on the keyboard.

"Please, sweetness, the pills first," he begged. "Once you get hold of Barty, things could happen really fast. I just don't want you to be distracted and forget . . ."

"Oh, all right," Mary Jo snapped. She lifted her skirt and extracted the pills from where they were tucked under the duct tape. "Here's your moldy old pills," and she tossed them at Smore.

"Nooooo," he shrieked, and lunged for the airborne pills, almost throwing himself off the sleigh in the process. He managed to catch them and haul himself back into the sleigh. "Thank you, thank you," he blubbered, his eyes on the black pills in his palm.

"What's that?" Mary Jo asked him, pointing at the horizon. "That big yellow thing? Do you see it?"

Mikhail squinted into the distance. His eyes widened and he moaned. "The busss," he hissed. He fell to the floor of the sleigh and began groveling and praying to every deity he could remember.

Mary Jo squinted into the distance too. "Why, it *is* a bus," she said. "A big old yellow school bus, and Barty's driving it!" The bus flew closer and Mary Jo squinted harder. "Are those *people* under the bus?" she wondered, then laughed. "I hope there's room for this big fat moron!" She kicked Mikhail in the side, but her foot sank ankle-deep in blubber and never reached his ribs.

The bus flew closer as the laptop monitor sprang to life and played the vid of 'President Zobama's Under My Bus'. Mary Jo hummed along with the song as Mikhail Smore trembled and squealed in terror.

Chapter 45
Rescue

Klaxons sounded throughout Bunker II. At the same moment, Ned's phone began to ring shrilly. Monitors flashed RED ALERT as a computer-generated voice appraised them of the situation.

"Warning, warning, red alert," said the voice. "Enemy spotted within ten miles of this location." The voice gave the coordinates. "The bus is rolling. Repeat: the bus is rolling! Man your stations," the voice continued. "Czars have been spotted! WE THE PEOPLE and the pilots have been notified. The Bald Eagles are flying! WARNING, all hell is breaking loose!"

Ned snapped open his phone, listened and turned back to the group. "We need transportation!" he exclaimed. "We have to try to get to Mary Jo before the bus does! The chopper is on its way back, but I don't think we'll make it in time!"

"Take the turnip truck," said Cookie. "It was just returned to Bay 2."

"We've got to *fly*," Ned explained. "What else do you have?"

"Take the turnip truck," urged Cookie. "It's all gassed up with the right kind of fuel and ready to go. It'll take you just as high as need be."

"Thanks," said Ned, and grabbed Chad's arm. "Let's roll, sport." They ran through the doors and started down the hall.

"WAIT!" yelled Dog. "Don't forget Ronny!" He grabbed the Ray-Gun from the gun rack and tossed it to Ned.

"Thanks, Dog," Ned yelled as he caught the gun. He and Chad ran down the hall, around a corner and through another doorway that led to Bay 2. There, under a spotlight, sat the turnip truck.

Ned and Chad looked dubiously at each other, then got into the cab.

"Not bad, not bad at all," said Ned, as he patted the oak dash and caressed the tucked and pleated red leather upholstery. "Let's see what this baby's got under the hood." He fired it up and the engine settled to a smooth and powerful roar. The huge bay doors opened to the outside as Ned familiarized himself with the controls. "Seems simple enough," he said. "Like a regular truck, except for this red button here . . .!" He pushed it and the turnip truck shot through the bay doors and into the night sky like a rocket. "YEE-HAW," yelled Ned.

The turnip truck soon leveled off and Ned punched in the coordinates. "Buckle up, sport," he told Chad, as he did the same. "We're in for a bumpy ride."

Chad looked out the side windows, then did a double take. The turnip truck was surrounded by Bald Eagles, war arrows clenched in their talons. Their eyes glittered fiercely as they searched the sky for the bus. "Wow," Chad thought, "I'm sure glad they're on our side!" He turned back to Ned with a question. "What's the plan? Do you have a plan, because I sure don't!"

"The plan is," said Ned, "to do whatever we have to. We'll try to swoop in and grab her right out of the sleigh while the Eagles attack the bus."

A few minutes later the lead Eagle gave a piercing shriek as he spotted the bus. The bus was aimed at the circling sleigh, it's trajectory making a head-on collision a certainty.

"He's going to throw Mary Jo under the bus along with Smore!" Chad exclaimed. "Why, that dirty, low-down . . .!" Chad shook his head. "We've got to save her. If that means saving Smore too, I guess that's the price we have to pay."

"Not necessarily," replied Ned. He pointed Ronny Ray-Gun at the sleigh and fired. The clones straightened out and the sleigh headed north. The Eagles attacked the bus, screaming their war cry. They pelted the bus with a storm of arrows and guano. Soon the bus was covered with guano and arrows were stuck all over it. Arrows had deflated the tires and cracked the windows. It was impossible for the bus driver to stay on target. Soon the bus began veering to the left – yes, even more to the left! As it wandered harmlessly off course, the Eagles returned to the battle taking place between the sleigh and the turnip truck.

"I will not ride in a turnip truck!" Mary Jo yelled as Chad tried to toss her a rope. "You can't make me! What would my friends say? LOOK!" she pointed to the south. "Barty's coming to get me right now!"

"Mary Jo," yelled Chad, "you don't have any friends! And Barty's not coming to get you. *You* look!" he exclaimed, pointing to the retreating bus and handing the rope to Ned.

"Barty!" called Mary Jo plaintively. "Barty!"

"He's gone," Chad yelled to her. "We're here to help you, and we're *not* from the government! Grab that rope!" he ordered her, as Ned threw it again. Mary Jo threw it back.

"I won't," screamed Mary Jo. "If Barty doesn't want me anymore, I don't want to live!" She stooped to the floor of the sleigh and began to search Mikhail Smore's pockets. "Give me those black pills, you moron! I need them! I can't live without Barty and without my kool-aid. You give them back, they should be mine!"

She shook his unresponsive bulk. His head rolled to the side and she saw the black foam on his lips.

"AARRGGHH!" she screamed, and attempted to throw herself out of the sleigh. Ned lassoed her in mid-aid and he and Chad began to haul her, kicking and screaming, into the turnip truck.

Chapter 46
Captured

"I don't know why there are fur-lined handcuffs in the back of this turnip truck," said Ned, as he fastened them around Mary Jo's wrists. "I'm just gonna adopt a 'don't ask, don't tell' policy on this one and try to forget I ever saw them."

"I think they're actually shackles," said Chad, "since they're attached to the truck. There's some for her ankles too." Chad and Ned quickly secured Mary Jo with the shackles, despite all her kicking and screaming.

"She's a regular spitfire, sport," Ned told Chad.

"I don't know what's wrong with her," Chad said. "She's never been like this before."

"Oh no," Ned groaned. "Look at her eyes! They're blue!"

"Yeah," said Chad, "she has blue eyes. So what?"

"No, sport, I mean *blue*!" Ned said. "No white of the eye, no black pupil, just all *BLUE*!" Ned snatched back his hands as Mary Jo snapped and snarled and tried to bite him. "Do you think we should use this thing here?" he asked Chad, holding up a rubber ball on a leather strap. Chad turned to look.

"Put that down!" he said. "She'll be okay, won't you Mary Jo? Mary Jo?" She continued to spit and snarl. "Her eyes!" exclaimed Chad. "You're right, they're entirely blue!" Mary Jo's electric blue kool-aid eyes flashed like lasers. "What's happening to her?" he asked, as they got back into the truck's cab.

"I think it's kool-aid withdrawal, sport," said Ned. "She was on some pretty strong stuff. I've never seen anyone this bad before. Brace yourself, sport. She may not recover."

"No!" said Chad. "She'll be fine! Can't we give her more kool-aid? Maybe some of that sleeping stuff too? Would that work?"

"Well, that might work, but we don't have any of that stuff," Ned told him.

"So what do we do now?" Chad asked. "What's the plan? We're in Canada again, do we just fly this turnip truck up to Alaska and find Rogue Peyton? Will Mary Jo survive the trip without kool-aid?" Chad frowned worriedly.

"I don't really have a plan, sport," said Ned.

"You don't have a plan?" Chad was dismayed. "Why not?"

"Things kind of went to hell in a handbasket real sudden, if you didn't notice." Ned was miffed. "I was going to call the chopper back, try to grab your girlfriend. After that . . . well, I meant to ask Cookie and the Bunker folks if they had any ideas, but I didn't get a chance . . ."

"But no," Chad sneered. "You had to goof off and drink Bunkertinis and play 'The Star-Spangled Banner' with that Dog person!"

"Hey, back off, sport," Ned told him. "I don't hear any brilliant plans coming from you! And anyway, playing the Anthem put the Eagles at attention, so they got in the air as soon as the alert sounded. Look, on the plus side, we've got your girlfriend, so that's taken care of . . ."

"Yes, but you don't have any supplies and she's in bad shape. We can't take her to the Bunker," Chad said.

"Yeah," Ned answered, "those are minuses. And the Czars are reactivated, and we're too close to the Gulag they're building, so we can't stay airborne." He banged his head lightly against the steering wheel as Mary Jo began to howl at the moon.

Suddenly a voice came through the truck's radio, loud and clear.

"Ned," yelled Dog. "Get out of the air now! The Czars have your location and they're homing in. WE THE PEOPLE are right on their butts, but the Czars won't engage them, they're after *you*!" Dog gave them coordinates. "Take that truck down *NOW*! I'll contact you when it's clear."

"Can someone bring kool-aid?" Chad pleaded, but the radio was silent.

"*HANG ON!*" Ned yelled, as he gunned the turnip truck's engine and took them into a nose dive.

Chapter 47
Thunder Road

The turnip truck made a hard landing on a rough and rocky road, barely wide enough to accommodate it.

"Ow," moaned Chad, who'd hit his head as the truck landed. "Take it easy, will you?" he said to Ned. He turned to look at Mary Jo, still secured in the back of the truck. "Oh, no," he exclaimed, "I think she's bleeding!" He began to get out of the truck.

"Wait," said Ned, 'let's find some cover first." He looked around the area. "No sense in making it easy for the Czars to find us, let's get this truck under that outcropping of rock." He pointed to a massive cliff nearby.

Soon the truck was tucked under the overhanging cliff. The Czars' black helicopters searched furiously overhead. The Eagles circled one location, then another, laying down a false trail. The Czars followed the Eagles, hoping they'd lead them to the turnip truck.

Ned assessed the situation. "Delaying tactics," he told Chad. "The Eagles are keeping the Czars in the area until WE THE PEOPLE get here to engage them in battle."

"They should lead them away from us," said Chad. "We're pinned down here! Mary Jo needs help, and those birds are keeping the Czars right on top of us!"

"Give them time, sport," Ned said. "Those are smart birds. They know what they're doing. They're edging them a little closer to that Gulag all the time – see how they regroup to the east? And the Czars follow them because they think the Eagles are guarding our position. I wouldn't be surprised if the Eagles and WE THE PEOPLE have cooked up a little ambush for the Czars!" He looked through the back window at Mary Jo. "Better check her out, sport," he told Chad. "She's not looking so good."

Chad scrambled into the back of the truck. "Mary Jo, wake up, wake up," he said, as he gently shook her. "You're safe now, and we'll get you help just as soon as we can."

Mary Jo awoke with a snarl. "Get your mitts off me," she snapped. "Some rescue this is. I'm tied up in the back of a turnip truck! I don't want your help. Untie me *RIGHT THIS MINUTE! I WANT KOOL-AID!*"

Ned slid the truck's back window open. "Here," he held out a case to Chad, and motioned him closer. "It's a first aid kit. I found it in the glove box. You'd better stop that bleeding." Ned lowered his voice and Chad moved closer. "Take this flashlight and check out the color of that blood before you bandage her. It doesn't look red to me." Chad took the items and turned back to Mary Jo.

"Mary Jo, honey," he began, "I've got a first aid kit, I'll get you fixed right up . . ."

Mary Jo's electric blue eyes lasered into him as she growled. "Unless you've got kool-aid in that kit, I'm not interested. NOW UNTIE ME *RIGHT THIS SECOND!*" she screamed and struggled against the shackles.

Chad turned on the flashlight and drew back in horror as he saw that Mary Jo had a scalp wound that was profusely bleeding blue blood. She continued to spit and snarl and struggle against her restraints. Her head thrashed violently from side to side, flinging droplets of blue blood everywhere.

"This is bad, sport," Ned said, leaning through the back window."She looks like she's auditioning for a remake of 'The Exorcist'. Here," and he tossed Chad a towel, "wrap her up!"

Chad managed to wrap the towel around Mary Jo's head, turban-style. Mary Jo presented a disturbing jihadist image in the turban, smeared with blue blood and screeching out her hate. Ned and Chad looked at each other dubiously, and without another word, Chad removed the towel turban. He opened the first aid case and sighed in relief.

"There's kool-aid here," he told Ned, removing a syringe filled with the bright blue liquid. "I just hope there's a sedative in with it. I've never done this before," he admitted. "Do you think you could? Her arm's right up by you."

"Sure," said Ned. "I vaccinate my livestock myself. No problem, sport." He took the syringe and quickly and expertly injected the blue liquid into Mary Jo's arm. She immediately quieted. Her eyes closed and she slipped into a comatose state. Chad made her as comfortable as he could, using burlap sacks meant to hold turnips to bolster and buffer her.

"Now what?" Chad asked, as he climbed back into the cab. "any plan yet?"

"It looks like the coast is clear," said Ned. "I guess we could go as far as possible on this road. It's hardly a road at all, more like a wide game trail. And the snow is getting deep. But it heads in the right direction."

They heard a loud noise from the direction Ned was pointing. "That's a crash," said Chad. "Maybe a Czar's helicopter?"

"No," said Ned. "there's no flashing lights or sirens. Whatever it was, it was blacked out." He looked at Chad. "It could be almost anything, but we don't really have a choice. We can't go back, we have to go forward." He started the truck and they drove out from under the cliff. "Here," said Ned, and handed Chad Ronny Ray-Gun. "Ronny's on 'stun' right now. Press that button there," he pointed, "and Ronny turns lethal." Chad gingerly took the gun and peered ahead as Ned drove slowly. Soon they came upon the crash site. There were broken saplings and trash was strewn parallel to the track they traveled.

Chad cautiously turned the flashlight's beam on the crashed vehicle. "It's Mikhail Smore!" he exclaimed. "This doesn't look good. I don't think there are any survivors." He searched the scene with the flashlight. Mikhail Smore and the clones were limp and lifeless. Black foam was smeared around Smore's mouth. "Poisoned!" he exclaimed. "They're dead!"

"There's nothing we can do for them," said Ned. "We have to keep moving." They continued north.

The truck's radio cackled to life again. "Wildman, Wildman, are you there? Dog here, do you read me?"

"We hear you, Dog, 5 by 5," said Ned. "Good to hear your voice, we thought we were on our own. Got a plan for us?"

"Sure do," replied Dog. "Just sit back, relax and leave the driving to me." Ned took his hands off the steering wheel and Dog took over by remote control. "simple as flying a Predator drone," Dog told them, as he sat back in his command module at Bunker II and finessed the joystick. He pushed a few buttons and the turnip truck morphed into a moonshiner's car, with Mary Jo tucked into the spot where the 'shine usually rode. "I'll have you over the border in no time," he said, and proceeded to maneuver the vehicle through the maze of tiny tracks, trails, dry streambeds and other obstacles.

"Thunder Road," exclaimed Ned happily, "great song!" And he began to sing as the vehicle continued it's high-speed twisting and turning and Mary Jo slumbered on, undisturbed.

Chapter 48
Wildlife Watching

"**D**on't make any noise . . . be really quiet," Dog whispered from the radio. The engine noise quieted as the vehicle went into stealth mode. "My radar shows a large group of 'Progressives' about to cross the track you're on." The car drove off the road and stopped in a copse of trees, hidden from view. Ned and Chad watched the intersection ahead.

"Dog," whispered Ned, speaking to the radio, "there's a bunch of people standing around in the middle of the road, right in our path."

"They're 'Moderates'," Dog replied. "Don't worry about them. They'll be gone in a minute when the 'Progressives' come through. There's no strong convictions in the 'Moderate' group, so they just stand around in the middle. They're easy to sway and easy to fool, but their flip-flopping makes them pretty useless. No real convictions, you know. They just want to 'go along to get along', it's all self-interest with them.

"Here come the 'Progressives' now," said Ned.

"Observe radio silence," said Dog, and the radio shut down.

"Watch this, sport," Ned whispered, in the hushed and awed voice usually used by commentators stalking animals in the wild. "It's rare to view this elusive group in their natural habitat. They're masters of disguise and sneaky tricks. They'll attach themselves to an issue and take it over, make it their own, then twist it into something antiquated and repressive and harmful. Do you hear them?" he asked excitedly. "Here they come."

"Oh . . . my . . . God," Chad muttered, his jaw dropping. He stared at the intersection, transfixed by the whirling, swirling mass of fur, claws and teeth. He took a deep breath and snapped out of it. "They look like Tasmanian devils," he said.

"Yes, but they're 'Progressives'," said Ned, staring intently ahead. "Maybe 500 of them, from the sound of it." He turned to Chad. "We don't have enough firepower, sport. We'll have to let them go this time," he said in a normal voice. "They'll never hear us over the racket they're making. We're downwind and their eyesight's really, really bad. They can't see the mistakes of the past and they want to repeat them. They can't see the unintended consequences of their actions. They can't see *us*! C'mon . . . we can get closer!" He slapped Chad on the back.

"N-n-no thanks," said Chad, nervously. "I'm fine right where I'm at. Besides, we can't leave Mary Jo. Remember what happened last time we did?!" Chad kept an eye on the 'Progressives'. "Why are they like that?" he asked. "Why are they fighting with each other? What's that slimy stuff all over them? And where'd the 'Moderates' go?"

"So many questions," Ned chuckled. "Okay, sport, we've got time." He nodded at the 'Progressives' still thronging the intersection. "It'll take that pack awhile to get out of our way. Uncle Ned will tell you a story. Once upon a time . . ." he began.

Chapter 49
Lesson Learned

Some time later the stream of 'Progressives' had dwindled to a trickle.

"Wow," said Chad, stretching. "I had no idea. Let me see if I've got this straight."

"Remember," Ned told him, "I gave you the condensed version."

"Gee," said Chad, sarcastically. "Coulda fooled me." He pointedly looked at his watch. The car started up and returned to the road the 'Progressives' had just vacated.

"Okay," Dog's voice came from the speaker. "Looks like it's all clear ahead. Just sit back, relax and enjoy the ride. Leave the driving to me. Estimated time of arrival at transfer point is 23 minutes."

"Plenty of time," said Ned. "Let's see if you've got this 'Progressive' thing down."

"Well," Chad began, repeating what Ned had told him, "there have been three 'Progressive' movements before this one. They did some good, but a lot of bad things too . . ."

"Like Prohibition," Ned interrupted, "don't forget Prohibition. A bad thing. A very, very bad thing! And income tax! Another very, very bad thing!"

"Like Prohibition and income tax," Chad agreed, "and they began attempting social control by taking power away from elected officials and giving it to professional administrators, so the voice of WE THE PEOPLE was diminished. Just like what's happening now, with all these Czars that aren't accountable to the people's representatives."

"They distanced government from WE THE PEOPLE. They installed these elitist administrators, and insisted that WE THE PEOPLE were too stupid to know what was best for them, so it was up to the administrators to exert social control to keep them in line," he continued.

"Prohibition," Ned said, "and eugenics. Don't forget eugenics."

"Right," Chad continued, "social controls like that. And the power the elected officials allowed to be taken away wasn't theirs, they held it in trust for WE THE PEOPLE."

"Stole it!" Ned exclaimed. "'Progressives' double down dirty stole it right out from under their noses! Just like what's happening now with all these Czars!"

"So this fourth 'Progressive' movement, this modern one, builds on the stuff the 'Progressives' of the past did, but they want to take it way, way beyond that," Chad said. "They want total control of our lives. They want to apply social justice instead of equal justice. They want to take us back to the feudal system, but with the government as the feudal lords making all the decisions for their serfs and living large while the people suffer."

"Pretty good," Ned admitted. "But do you remember why the 'Progressives' we saw looked and acted the way they did?"

"I think so," said Chad. "Modern 'Progressives' are fractioned into a whole bunch of different causes, mainly social activism movements. Activist and political groups, media organizations, leftist fringe groups of all kinds. They promote I don't know what all – stuff like social democracy, left-liberalism, centrism, democratic socialism . . ."

"PETME, MoveAlong, Code Stink, Code Whack-A-Doo," Ned interrupted him. "So what do they all have in common?"

"They're elitist. They're motivated by money and power. And they want to change the status quo," Chad answered. "They want to go against what are considered traditional American values and beliefs. That's why they group together, but that's also why they fight so much amongst themselves. The different groups disagree on lots of stuff, but they try to get along to get bits and pieces of their agendas accomplished and to accumulate money and power. That sticky stuff on them glues different groups together on the issues they agree on. That's why one has its paw glued to another's butt while another's nose is in its ear."

"Don't forget their poor vision," Ned reminded him. "They don't see the future of their actions, don't see the unintended consequences and don't look to history to avoid repeating mistakes of the past. That's why they were mostly going backwards while fighting, and not looking where they were going. And some just flat out don't care if they destroy the country to get what they want."

"Many are Millennials," Ned continued. "Born between 1978 and 2000, products of our 'free', liberal-controlled public indoctri-nation, er, education system. Their textbooks lie, they've been taught that America is not great, they've been subjected to an extended adolescence and long-schooling, they've been told how wonderful they are virtually all their lives without ever having to prove it and they've been taught that their actions don't have consequences. When they run up against the real world they automatically figure the world is wrong because it doesn't conform to their artificial ideals, so they go about remaking the world and wind up with an artificial construct that is inherently destructive!

Because they have an incomplete education, they're easily fooled and don't know they're repeating mistakes of the past."

"Hey," laughed Chad, "that's *my* age group, too. We're not all like that."

"You, sport," Ned chuckled, "are a closet conservative who had ulterior motives for acting like a liberal that we've already discussed! You're right, though, not all Millennials are 'Progressives', but Millennials make up a large percentage of the current 'Progressive' movement."

The vehicle stopped where the road ended. Ahead was a field of deep snow with two snowmachines warmed up and ready. A bundled and muffled driver sat on one which was fitted with a litter for Mary Jo. As if on cue, Mary Jo moaned.

"Better give her another dose," Dog's voice came from the radio. "Take that first aid kit with you, just in case. Good luck to you all."

"Thanks for your help, Dog," said Chad. "You and all the Bunker folks. Mary Jo would want to thank you too, and apologize for her behavior."

Ned finished giving Mary Jo another kool-aid injection and tucked the first aid kit somewhere in his buckskins. He and Chad picked up Mary Jo and began carrying her towards the waiting snowmachines.

"Thanks, Dog," Ned called back to the vehicle, "don't forget hunting next week. We'll stock the Bunker freezers!"

"Vroom, vroom!" Dog gunned the engine in agreement. The vehicle turned around and sped back the way it had come.

Ned and Chad arrived at the snowmachines and strapped Mary Jo into the litter. The snowmachine driver pushed up his goggles and loosened his muffler.

"Dude Peyton!" Chad exclaimed.

"Here," Dude said, handing them goggles and cold weather gear. "Better bundle up."

Chapter 50
Setting a New Course

"You didn't answer one question," Chad told Ned as they put on the cold weather gear. "What happened to the 'Moderates'?"

"C'mon, sport, you're a bright boy. What happens when you stand in the middle of the road?" Ned asked him.

"Well, I guess you get run over," Chad answered.

"Bingo!" exclaimed Ned. "We have a winner!" He helped Chad with the communications gear, attaching a packset to his belt and running the coiled earpiece wire up to his ear.

"I feel just like the Secret Service!" Chad said. "Where's the microphone? Don't I have to talk into my wrist?"

"Nope," said Ned. "We fixed that after I almost cut my ear off. It's dangerous to talk into your wrist when you have a knife in your hand!" He showed him how to use the radio controls. "Let's test this stuff out. Just talk normal."

"Can you hear me now?" asked Chad.

"Sky King to Penny . . . Sky King to Penny," called Ned.

"Huh?" Chad replied.

"Sorry, sport, generational glitch," Ned answered. "Can you hear me now?"

"I hear you both 5 by 5," said another voice in their earpieces. "Let's get moving. Lot of miles ahead of us. Stay close and no radio chatter. Emergency use only. I laid down some false trails earlier. That might fool them for a while, give us a head start."

"Who's 'them'?" Chad asked Ned. "I thought it was smooth sailing from here."

"Cut the chatter," Dude's voice ordered in their ears. "Every battle delays us and diverts us from our objective. Weapons ready, but don't fire until my say so. Stay alert!"

"Eyes sharp, sport," Ned whispered as they headed west, "and don't forget to look up."

"Quiet!" Dude hissed.

The snowmachines ran silently on a northwest heading, twisting and turning and snaking through the trees on a barely discernible track. At times, Chad glimpsed another set of snowmachines, mirroring their route on a parallel course. He nudged Ned in the ribs and pointed at the doppelgangers. Ned nodded and placed his finger on his lips, warning Chad to be quiet. "Decoy," he silently mouthed. Chad nodded in understanding. Their machines, in stealth mode, ran swiftly and silently while the noisy decoys drew attention.

Soon a louder noise began to drown out the roar of the decoy snowmachines. It was actually a sequence of noises – first a maddening tap, tap, tap tapping, then a high-pitched whine that rose to a crescendo, followed by the sound of a rushing waterfall. That sound changed to a giant, sucking whirlpool noise. Next was a series of loud SPLAT, SPLAT, SPLATs. When those stopped, just as Chad thought it was over, a final GLUG, GLUG was heard. Then the sequence began anew.

It was Ned's turn to elbow Chad in the ribs and point. Chad peered into the distance. Ned handed him the field glasses. Chad looked intently. Suddenly his jaw dropped. His shaking hand lowered the field glasses to reveal eyes wide in shock. As he drew breath to speak, Ned clapped his hand over Chad's mouth, putting a finger to his own lips at the same time. Chad nodded feebly. Ned dropped his hands. "Buck up, sport," he mouthed, patting Chad on the back. Chad nodded again.

Suddenly the two sets of snowmachines began to converge. Chad braced himself, anticipating a collision. Instead, his machine and the one ahead dropped onto a ramp that led deep underground while the two decoy machines sped along in their place.

"Go ahead and talk," Dude's voice sounded in their ears. "They can't hear us here. I bet Sixpack has a question or two," he chuckled.

"Just a few," Chad agreed weakly.

Ned passed him the flask. "No thanks," said Chad. "I think I need to stay sharp."

Ned put the flask away. "Okay, sport," he said. "Lucy, I got some 'splainin' to do." He pulled out a bag and handed Chad an energy bar. "Here, got to keep your energy up. I made them myself." Chad took one and looked at Ned pointedly, waiting for him to begin explaining the monstrous thing he'd just seen in the sky.

Ned drew a deep breath. "Okay . . ." he began.

Chapter 51
Eyewitness

". . . why don't we start with you telling me what you thought you saw?" Ned asked Chad.

"What I *thought* I saw? What I THOUGHT I saw? WHAT I *THOUGHT* I SAW?" Chad yelled.

"Whoa, sport,' Ned grimaced, yanking out his earpiece. "don't blow out our eardrums!"

"Hey," Dude's voice sounded in Chad's ear, "keep it down back there!"

"Sorry," said Chad. He looked at Ned closely. "You know what I saw. Don't try to tell me you didn't see the same thing."

"No, no, sport," said Ned hastily. "I saw it too. It's hard to put it into words, I just hoped you could do a better job of describing it for me. You know, you being so edu-ma-cated and all. Quietly, though," he requested, as he reinserted his earpiece.

"Okay," said Chad, sarcastically. "I'll describe it for you. It was a . . . a big . . . well, it was round, like a globe, like a light bulb? No, more like a huge ball."

"Like a sphere?" suggested Ned.

"Yes!" Chad agreed eagerly. "A sphere! And it was clear, wasn't it? But cloudy inside – black and red swirling clouds. And it was dirty, like dogs in a car smear the windows."

"Could you see anything inside the black and red clouds?" Ned queried.

"Yes!" Chad exclaimed. "I remember now – but it can't be, that's just too crazy . . ."

"Spill it, sport," Ned demanded, "we're not in Kansas anymore!"

"It was a toilet," said Chad, "a huge, white toilet set inside the sphere. And it flushed," he moaned, "oh my God, it flushed!" Chad rubbed his eyes and tried to erase the image.

"Did you see anything – *anyone* – in there with the toilet?" Ned asked him.

"Faces, there were faces. And fingers. Fingers like that old Dr. Phibes movie, you know, Vincent Price," he babbled nervously. "Like the murderer's hands transplanted onto that piano player," he continued. "Like dancing phalanges . . . the tapping," he moaned, "tap, tap, tapping . . . nevermore!" he gasped.

"Snap out of it, sport!" Ned shook him and smacked him lightly on the back of his head. "Eyes here," he said, pointing two fingers at Chad's eyes, then at his own. "The big bad sphere is following the decoys, not us. We're safe."

"But, the decoys," Chad protested, "SPLAT!"

"Remote controlled, no one got SPLATTED . . . this time," Ned told him. "Relax and Uncle Ned will explain it all." He grabbed a bottle of water and handed one to Chad. "'Splainin' is thirsty work," he said, and took a big gulp. He leaned back and got comfortable while the snowmachine continued on course, controls slaved to Dude's machine ahead.

"That, sport," Ned told Chad, "was the Far-Left Blogosphere."

"You mean . . ." Chad motioned at the snowmachine ahead, "Mary Jo?"

"Oh, no," Ned said, "although I'm sure she'd have gotten there soon. She's been what they call a disruptor – she disrupts an existing conservative blog. She doesn't have her own blog yet, does she? That's the next step. That and contributing to the far left blogs."

"No," Chad assured him. "She just goes on that one conservative blog. She tried others, but now she concentrates her efforts."

"That's good, she's not too far gone," Ned told him. "That tap-tap-tapping you hear are all the bloggers in the Far-Left Blogosphere flinging the poo. They spin it, make it up, it's lies and innuendo and conjecture twisted into 'truth', it's bogus facts and fancies and perceived slights. Those black and red clouds are it's aura – it's all anger, deceit and hate."

Ned fiddled with the field glasses, which had automatically snapped and saved all the images. He handed them to Chad.

"Look here," Ned said, pointing at the image of the sphere. "See all those faces and fingers? That's what's smeared the inside of the thing. Chad looked, and saw faces pressed against the sphere, screaming, drooling and foaming at the mouth. Their fingers incessantly tapped out their rage and lies. Chad shuddered and turned away.

"And the poo goes . . .?" Chad asked.

"Right into the crapper," Ned told him. "That high-pitched noise like a blender is them spinning it. Then the waterfalling and whirlpooling and flushing and SPLAT SPLAT, then GLUG GLUG and then they do it all over again." Ned whistled a few bars of a familiar tune. "Reminds me of a song," he mused. "Plop, plop, fizz, fizz . . ."

"Ah, excuse me for interrupting," said Chad, "but what are they doing with the poo?"

"They throw poo bombs," Ned explained. "flushed down the toilet and aimed at anyone who objects to the far left agenda.

People they see as a threat. Right now that's Rogue Peyton. The far left invented BDS – that's Bush Derangement Syndrome – to keep the liberal base in line. They've indoctrinated them so thoroughly that now all they have to do is mention Bush and the base goes crazy. They focus on hatred of Bush and don't see what a radical agenda this administration and the majority in Congress are following. Sleight of hand, misdirection, whatever you want to call it, it's used to control their own people. The effect of BDS on conservatives is wasted time trying to reason with a liberal who has the syndrome."

"So what's a conservative to do? Just ignore someone with BDS?" Chad asked him.

"You got it, sport," said Ned. "Ignore them or point out that Bush is history and we need to deal with the here and now."

"So they're flinging the poo at Rogue Peyton instead of Bush?" Chad wanted to know.

"Worse than that, sport," Ned told him. "they're trying to transfer BDS to her. Change it into PDS – Peyton Derangement Syndrome. What you didn't see, on the ground back there, were the hordes of so-called 'investigative' reporters and private eyes hired by the far left to dig up anything they can on her. Funny thing is, the Far-Left Blogosphere flushes the poo and the 'investigative' types spend their time investigating it and finding nothing. The Far-Left Blogosphere wants to make Peyton waste time and money and effort defending herself against the smears. They want to overwhelm her with attacks from all sides."

"HA!" exclaimed Dude's voice through their earpieces. "If they think they can overwhelm my wife, they don't know her at all! You'd better wrap up the explanation, we'll be there soon."

"Where?" Chad wanted to know.

"Oh, and I'm afraid your girlfriend is waking up," Dude continued. "Be prepared for a fight."

"Oh, no," Chad moaned, and dropped his head into his hands.

"Buck up, sport," Ned encouraged him. "The end is near. Now is no time to quit!" The snowmachines began to ascend a ramp.

Chapter 52
Arrival

The ramp led to a huge garage. The snowmachines came to a stop and the men dismounted. Mary Jo remained strapped in the back of Dude's snowmachine. She was fully awake, spitting and snarling and howling for kool-aid.

"Can't we give her more kool-aid?" Chad asked.

"Shhhh," Dude replied. "She doesn't know who we are. Don't take off the cold weather gear yet and don't let her hear your voice. It'll be easier that way."

"But . . ." Chad began.

"And no more kool-aid," Dude whispered. "The less she has in her system, the better the red pill works."

"KIDNAPPED!" shrieked Mary Jo, "kidnapped *again*! Who are you guys? I'm warning you bunch of grease monkeys, I'm important! I have friends in high places! *Very* high places, if you know what I mean! Get me out of this sled!"

The three men looked at each other and shrugged. Dude walked to a nearby computer station and wheeled back a big red leather chair. Mary Jo looked at the chair, then at Dude. Her eyes narrowed and glittered dangerously.

"No way," she spat, "no way am I getting into that chair!"

The three men looked at each other again. "Watch her teeth," warned Ned, as they grabbed Mary Jo and gently wrestled her into the chair. They quickly attached her restraints to the chair and began to wheel her toward the elevator. Instead of entering the elevator, Dude directed the chair to a door next to it. It opened into a small room similar to a college dorm room. Dude removed one restraint from Mary Jo's wrist. Leaving her to undo the rest, the men quickly exited the room.

"She'll be safe in there," Dude told them. "It'll be easier once she's calmed down some."

"But that's the problem," Chad said, "she won't calm down without the kool-aid!"

Dude pulled a curtain and revealed a window into Mary Jo's temporary abode. "One-way mirror," he said. They saw that Mary Jo had removed the remaining restraints. She'd opened the refrigerator and found a big pitcher full of bright blue kool-aid. She was gulping it greedily from the pitcher. As they watched, she lowered the pitcher to reveal a big blue Joker's smile. She belched, put the pitcher back in the refrigerator and sat quietly on the side of the bed.

"I thought you said no more kool-aid," Chad said accusingly, glaring at Dude.

"That's not the kind of kool-aid she's used to," Dude told him. "No special blue pill ingredients in that stuff, just water, sugar, blue coloring and raspberry flavoring."

"But she calmed down," said Chad. "She only calms down with that special kool-aid!"

"Paxton!" Dude called out. "I know you're still here. I need your help explaining something."

"Be right there, Daddy," a small voice answered him.

"This is Pax's doing," Dude told them. "She can explain it best."

Paxton stepped around a corner. Her small frame was neatly covered with a miniature white lab coat. Tortoise-shell half-spectacles were perched on her nose and she carried a clipboard. She ran to hug her father, then turned to the other two men.

"Hello," she greeted them. "How may I be of assistance?" The men were removing hats, mufflers, masks and goggles. Paxton peered intently over her spectacles. "Uncle Ned!" she shrieked, and ran to hug him.

"Paxton!" exclaimed Ned happily. "How's my favorite little Lab Rat? Care to go hunting next week with me and Dog?"

"That's Lab *Princess*!" Paxton corrected him, "not Lab Rat! I can't go next week. Mama is taking me fishing on the big boat!"

"Well, you can't miss a date with Mama," Ned told her. He turned to Chad. "Paxton, let me introduce Chad Sixpack. It's his girlfriend, Mary Jo, who's in your cute little room right now."

"Hello," Paxton said to Chad, "pleased to meet you. I'm sorry about your girlfriend. My Mama will help her get better."

"It's a pleasure to meet you, Paxton," said Chad. "I sure hope your Mama can help Mary Jo. Your Daddy said you helped her to calm down."

"I fooled her," said Paxton. "I helped her mind calm her down by making her think she got the special kool-aid. The walls are blue like the sky, and that makes her calmer too. The music in there is Mozart. Her heart will slow down to beat in time with it." She flipped open a metal box mounted on the wall, adjusted a dial and flipped a switch. "Now she's smelling jasmine and getting calmer. Pretty soon she'll get sleepy and I'll dial in roses to give her nice dreams."

"Paxton, you're brilliant," exclaimed Chad. "Could I do this at home?"

Just then an urgent ringing was heard. Paxton pulled out her phone and read what she'd just been texted. "Uh-oh," she told her father. "Mama's in the gym."

"Nothing was scheduled," protested her father.

"E-MER-GEN-CY," Paxton enunciated carefully, reading the text.

Dude rushed to the elevator, followed closely by Ned and Chad.

Chapter 53
Game's On

The elevator doors opened and Dude rushed them through the lobby. They heard muffled crowd noise beyond closed double doors leading to the gym. Dude led them through another door, through the locker room and through the players' entrance to the sidelines, where his older daughters waited.

"What's up?" he asked them. "Pax said it was an emergency. Was it a sneak attack?"

"Not really," replied his eldest daughter. "Mom knew he'd try something after that bus thing. She," pointing at her sister, "was to tell Paxton 'NOT an emergency'. She *texted* her!"

"My bad," her sister replied. "I forgot to put in NOT. Won't happen again. Promise!"

"Just don't surprise us like that," their father said. "And better tell Paxton it was a false alarm. She's entertaining a guest." He introduced Chad. "Chad's girlfriend, Mary Jo, is resting in Pax's relaxation room."

The sisters looked at each other. "We'll both go," they said as one, then hurriedly left the gym, eager to see Mary Jo for themselves.

"Don't disturb her," their father called after them. The girls waved and blew kisses as they disappeared into the locker room.

The men turned their attention to the action in the middle of the gym. A lone figure, attired in fencing gear, faced a giant monitor.

Barty glared out from the monitor. A shadowy, menacing figure was behind him, using a joy stick to control his moves. Barty had chosen to wear his suit, sans jacket, and had even kept his tie on. He'd chosen fencing, then tried to cheat by insisting that he could legally substitute a light saber for a foil. Unfortunately, light sabers don't really exist, so his weapon of choice was actually a *plastic toy* light saber. He jabbed awkwardly with it, but the figure in dazzling white parried every attempt. Barty tried to jump back, but the slick soles of his expensive shoes slipped on the gym floor and he landed hard on his butt. His opponent lunged and thrust and suddenly the match was over. Barty faded to a blurred image and the monitor went dark. The fencer took off the mask and shook out long auburn hair. She saluted the stands with her foil and WE THE PEOPLE cheered. Dude went to meet his wife as she walked off the gym floor.

"I know, I know" Ned said to Chad. "You need an explanation. Let's find someplace quiet. WE THE PEOPLE will be hitting the refreshments in the lobby. How about the mens locker room?" Without waiting for a reply, Ned led the way.

"Okay, sport," said Ned, as they sat on the locker room benches, "here's the deal. It's Wii. The whole gym is Wii. 100th generation, or something like that – way, way advanced. So the Salesman says something like 'there's no deathcare panels in the healthcare bill' and Rogue points out chapter and verse where there are deathcare panels. Then he gets all we-weed and they Wii it out, him in DC, her here in this ultra-secret facility."

"Wow," Chad said, "that's incredible. Will it be on the market soon? Can I get one now?"

"Focus, Chad, focus" Ned told him, once again pointing at Chad's eyes, then his own. "This is like mega-secret military stuff, so your lips better be zipped and locked." He pantomimed zipping, locking and throwing away the key on his own lips.

"Okay," said Chad, regretfully. "Do you think I could maybe play it sometime?"

"Oh, sure," said Ned. "Any of WE THE PEOPLE can play it! Freedom of speech, right to challenge our government and all that. Speak up, speak out, speak loud and proud! It's your duty and your responsibility to participate in our country's government. Any time, sport, any time."

"Well, I'm not very good at fencing," Chad said.

"Doesn't have to be fencing," Ned said. "Rogue's played him at tennis, martial arts, swimming, lacrosse, tiddlywinks, polo, I can't remember them all. There's a list in the gym if you're interested. What he won't play her at is basketball. We think he'll be forced to go one-on-one with her by 2012, though."

"What do I do?" Chad asked. "Do I pick a sport . . . or?"

"Sign up over there," Ned pointed to a tablet computer hanging on the wall. Chad walked over to it and picked up the stylus to add his name to the list. He gasped, then laughed and turned to Ned.

"This list has millions of names on it," he said. "I'll be dead before I get to the top."

"Not necessarily, sport," Ned assured him. "Write letters, email and call your elected officials, at all levels, you'll move up on the list. Demand clearness and transparency and accountability. Vote in every election, but be informed about the candidates and issues. Run for local office, national office, move up on the list. Likewise if you have a blog or radio show or audience of some kind. Or if you root out corruption. Be true to WE THE PEOPLE, arm yourself with the facts and you'll be surprised how far you'll go. That's what Rogue did. Trust me on this, Chad, you got to start out playing the small clubs before you fill the big arena."

"Okay," Chad said, "I'll do it!" And he added his name to the list.

"Good for you, sport," Ned told him. "Now here's a tough question. Do we stick around and watch the next match? It's Heck against the Salesman, battling it out about all the Czars. They're firewalking! Or do we get back down below and see about your girlfriend getting that red pill?"

"Mary Jo!" Chad exclaimed, and sprang to his feet.

Chapter 54
Waiting Room

Ned and Chad took the elevator back downstairs. When the doors opened, they saw the three sisters intently peering through the window at Mary Jo. Chad rushed over and Ned followed.

"Is she okay?" Chad asked the girls.

"She's fine," Paxton replied, "she slept for awhile, then she drank more kool-aid. She's getting bored now. Short attention span, I'd guess."

Ding! The elevator doors opened again and Rogue and Dude stepped out.

"Chad," Rogue exclaimed, "it's a pleasure to meet you! Mary Jo is so blessed to have you. Many men would have walked away from a political kool-aid junkie girlfriend. But you chose to undertake a long and dangerous journey to try to break her addiction." Rogue hugged him warmly.

"Th-th-thanks," Chad stammered, "I'm kind of overwhelmed . . . I never thought . . . and meeting you . . . and all these other important, busy people all helping me . . . and Mary Jo . . . I don't know what to say . . . 'thank you' doesn't seem like enough."

"'Thank you' is plenty for all of us who've helped you," she replied. "We're WE THE PEOPLE, and that's what WE THE PEOPLE DO – we help each other and ourselves without waiting around for the government to try to do it for us!" She chuckled, then grew serious. "But your country wants more from you. Your country *needs* more from you. America is an idea, and do you know what that idea needs to succeed? It needs the active and informed participation of its citizens!"

"I know," Chad said, "I signed up for Wii, and I intend to take my responsibilities as a citizen seriously!"

"There you go, then," said Rogue, "you're already on the right track." She patted Chad on the back approvingly. "Why don't you have a seat over there," she pointed to a cozy seating area where her youngest played with blocks, "while I visit with Mary Jo for a bit. I'll probably call you in later."

"I don't know if that's a good idea," Chad said, looking worried. "She's been on that kool-aid for a long time, and certain people set her off pretty bad. I'm sorry, but you're one of them."

"No problem," Rogue said confidently. She fiddled with her hair, switched her glasses and suddenly became Nina Spay. "I'll just wear camouflage, like any hunter would." She laughed at Chad's expression. "Joking!" she exclaimed, changing hair and glasses and becoming herself again. "No 'bait and switch' tactics here – that's the Salesman's area of expertise! Lighten up, Chad! This isn't gloom and doom, it's awakening and enlightenment. We'll celebrate after it's all over," she assured him. She gave him a little shove toward the seating area. "Go on, Mary Jo and I are going to have a little girl talk." She looked at him sharply. "When's the last time you ate anything? Never mind. Dude," she called to her husband, "make sure he eats!" She joined her daughters at the window briefly, then stepped into Mary Jo's temporary lair.

Ned and Chad settled in comfortable chairs. The area was outfitted with a mini kitchen and refrigerator, and Dude handed out sandwiches and other refreshments before joining his son in block play on the carpet.

"Dude," Ned said, munching on a sandwich, "me and Dog are going hunting next week. Want to go with?"

"Can't," he replied, "family fishing trip. What are you hunting?"

"Hollyweird types," Ned told him. "Ahhnold RINO, Mat Demon, Brawn Penncil Dic . . ."

"Gotcha," Dude interrupted him, placing his hands over his son's ears and glancing toward his daughters.

"Sorry," Ned said, "forgot about the little ears."

"Time for his nap anyway," Dude said, standing and scooping up his son in the same motion. "If I don't see you again, Chad, it was a pleasure to meet you. Good luck to you and your Mary Jo."

"Thank you," Chad said, "I wish there was some way to repay you for everything you've done for us."

"Just stay true to WE THE PEOPLE," Dude replied, "and to the Republic." He headed for the elevator.

"This might take a little time," Ned told Chad, "press that button on the side of your chair," he said, while pressing the button on his own chair. The chairs reclined. "May as well catch a few zzzzzs." He pressed buttons on a remote control unit and the lights dimmed. Ned closed his eyes and almost immediately began to snore softly.

Chad tried to relax, but found it difficult. He tossed and turned and squirmed. When he finally drifted off, his sleep was fitful and fraught with nightmares. Chad moaned and groaned and tried to wake up, but he was stuck firmly in the nightmare, presented with a terrifying vision of the future of the Republic.

Chapter 55
Party Crasher

Chad dreamed he was in a Hollyweird movie – and that he was the star of the movie. He was taken to a place – by limo – a big White House. He was taken through the door and into a room cluttered with the glitterati. He saw the famous and the foolish, often one and the same. They scraped and bowed and fawned over an imperial figure seated on a throne. A footman Marine, clad in electric blue satin knee breeches and wearing a powdered wig, approached Chad.

"Sir," he said, "your invitation, please." Chad looked down at his hand and saw the formal invitation there. He also saw that he was attired in a tuxedo and that his face was reflected in his highly-polished shoes! He noticed a small, exquisitely wrapped gift in his other hand. He offered it to the footman.

"Oh no, sir," the footman said. "You'll be able to present it yourself in . . . oh, I'd say about three hours," he said, consulting his watch for the time, then expertly scanning the crowd. "Just step to the back of the line there." He pointed to an elegantly dressed couple nearby. Their backs were to the entryway, but as Chad walked over to stand behind them, they turned to each other and he recognized the Hollyweird power couple standing patiently, awaiting their turn.

Chad slept on while his brain screamed for him to wake up and end the nightmare.

"No-no-no," he muttered, his head thrashing from side to side. "Wake up, wake up – this isn't real. Help," he called faintly. Ned snored on, sleeping deeply and undisturbed.

Chad froze in disbelief as the nightmare unfolded. His breathing shallowed and became labored.

"Hello, there," the woman said to Chad as he took his place behind her and her escort. "I'm . . ."

"I know who you are," Chad said. "I'm just so surprised to meet you. I . . . um . . . um . . . I guess I don't know what to say!"

"Believe me, we understand completely," said the woman. "So many fans are tongue-tied when they meet us!" She and her escort laughed companionably. "You may call us by our first names. No need to stand on ceremony! But who are you, and why don't we know you? This event is pretty exclusive, and we know . . ." she looked around the room, ". . . almost everyone here. You, however, are quite the mystery man!" She tucked her hand into Chad's elbow and moved closer, as her husband looked on. "So tell, tell, tell!" she demanded gleefully.

"Well, my name is . . ." Chad thought desperately, ". . . Mikhail Smore!" he stated with relief. "I don't know why I'm here. Maybe a mixup? Did they want the documentary filmmaker? And got me instead? All I know," Chad said, feeling more confident with his story, "is that if you get invited, you show up! Do we really get to meet the Big Guy himself?" He nodded toward the throne.

"That explains it," the woman whispered to her husband. "I guess the administration is still having trouble vetting people. We should complain." She turned back to Chad. "I see you've brought a gift. I just hope it's something appropriate. And your Pledge?"

"Pledge?" Chad queried.

"Yes, the Pledge," she said. "We were just arguing about ours. I want to pledge to be a surrogate mother for Obantam's child. He," she motioned to her husband, "wants to pledge his twelve-year old as a slave. Reparations for slavery in the past, you know."

The orchestra began playing a new selection. The crowd, recognizing the tune, laughed and applauded and began chanting.

"Mmm, mmm, mmm . . .

Mmm, mmm, mmm . . .

Mmm, mmm, mmm . . ."

All of a sudden giant spotlights lit up an area just outside the floor-to-ceiling windows and sets of paned double doors. A red carpet, replete with a forest of microphones, was revealed.

"Ohhhhhh," sighed the crowd, adoringly, and headed for the doors. The celebrities flocked to the carpet and basked in the blazing lights. They jostled for position in front of the microphones and generally acted charming and clueless. Soon the big room was empty except for Chad, the footmen and the throned figure. The figure motioned for Chad to approach, which he did with trepidation, as the footmen Marines flanked him.

"Sooooo . . .," Obantam said, slouching on the throne, "you're not the usual celebrity. You're not drawn to the bright lights. Are you immune or what?" he asked suspiciously."Or an infiltrator from the Resistance?"

"I'm not a celebrity," Chad stated, then added bravely, "but I'm surprised you're not out there!"

"I don't share the spotlight," Obantam said petulantly, and I have my own personal media. Actually, *all* the media!" He chuckled, then frowned. "Except Cox, of course." He nodded to the scene outside. "I'll make them pay for their desertion, and I may reward you for your loyalty." He chuckled again. "It depends on the gift you've brought me. Everyone's been giving me the same gift, and I'm bored with it." He picked up a handful of jeweled pins depicting his omnipresent 'O' symbol and tossed them aside. "What have you got for me?" Chad timidly held out the gift. Obantam ripped off the bow and paper and opened the box. Inside was a small American flag pin, enameled red, white and blue. Obantam threw the pin angrily to the floor and ground his heel on it. "That's all over with," he snarled, "past, gone and forgotten. There's a New World Order now. That symbol is banned. I could have you executed right here, right now. I think I'll do that, unless you've got one heck of a Pledge for me." He scowled at Chad.

"P-p-p-pledge?" stammered Chad.

"Yes, Pledge," Obantam told him. "You know, the Pledge that a couple of those Hollynuts," he gestured to the celebrities crowding the red carpet outside, "started way back when. What you'll do for me! THE *PLEDGE*!" he yelled.

"Pledge," said Chad, placing his hand over his heart. "I Pledge Allegiance to the Flag of the United States of America, and to the Republic . . ."

"STOP!" screamed Obantam, jumping to his feet, his crown askew. "FORBIDDEN! BANNED! Guards! Guards! Bring me a gun! No, bring me a *MACHETE*!"

". . . for which it stands, One Nation, Under God, Indivisible, with Liberty and Justice for All!" Chad finished in a rush, and stepped back.

Just then a volley of gunshots rang outside. The celebrities on the red carpet began dropping, sliced with shrapnel, their blood turning the red carpet even redder. A percussive explosion blew out every window and glass door along the wall, opening the room to the outside. Obantam fell on his butt, right on the American flag pin. The upraised pin stuck him firmly in the left butt cheek as he scuttled under the throne. The footmen clapped their hands over their ears, wincing from the pain. Chad saw his opportunity and took it. He ran to the bank of shattered windows and dove through the nearest, flattened himself against the outside wall and skirted the carnage on the carpet.

Chapter 56
Girl Talk

Mary Jo stood when she heard the door begin to open, ready to attack. When she saw who entered, she began to shriek and scream, spit and sputter and claw at the air. She was on her way to a full-fledged meltdown when Rogue closed the door, snapped her fingers and pointed at Mary Jo.

"That'll be enough of that," she commanded. "Sit down and calm yourself. You're in my house and I insist on civilized behavior. You and I have important things to discuss." Mary Jo, shocked into good behavior, sat down and shut her mouth. She folded her arms and glared at Rogue, who leaned casually against the counter and gazed serenely back at her.

"First let's get a few things straight," she told Mary Jo. "You don't know me. What you think you know about me is from untrustworthy sources. You haven't been doing your due diligence and rooting out the facts. I don't know you either. Most of what I know about you is in your own words, from your blogging, but I think that's the kool-aid talking. I don't know the *real* Mary Jo, any more than you know the *real* Rogue. So try to set aside your bias and help us sort things out." Mary Jo unfolded her arms and relaxed a bit.

"Why am I here?" Mary Jo asked sullenly. "Did you have me kidnapped? Where's Chad? Is he in on this too?"

"You're here because your boyfriend, Chad, risked life and limb to get you here. That's how much he cares about you. After everything he went through to get you and me together in this room, don't you think you at least owe him the courtesy of hearing what I have to say?"

Mary Jo shrugged. "Maybe," she replied, becoming agitated, "but what about everything *I've* been through? I was *kidnapped*, and Chad let it happen! He drugged me, he lost me, he tied me up . . ."

"He's the good guy here, Mary Jo. He did what he thought was best at the time," Rogue interrupted her, "and he always acted in what he thought to be your best interests. He acted honorably."

"Okay," said Mary Jo, after a short, silent staring contest. "I'll listen. What's so freaking important to you all?"

"Do you remember the Mary Jo you used to be?" Rogue asked her. "You know, the one before your very first political rally." She clicked a remote and a wall monitor came to life, showing Mary Jo in happier times, before the rally. "Then," Rogue continued, "you had your first sip of kool-aid. Sometimes, Mary Jo, all it takes is one time, and you're hooked, addicted and gone, baby, gone. Then a smooth-talking, hypnotic, flashy, trashy, manipulating, narcissistic Salesman can talk a political virgin into anything. Before you know what's happening, you're enslaved to the Beltway and selling yourself in ways you couldn't even imagine before you drank the kool-aid." Mary Jo watched, mesmerized, as the monitor showed the political rally, then switched to scenes featuring the rabid zombie she'd become. Images captured on cell phones and posted to youtube flashed in rapid succession as Mary Jo began to shake.

"An INTERVENTION?!" Mary Jo shrieked, jumping up. "This is an *intervention*? Chad thinks I need an *INTERVENTION*?!

I *changed*, that's all. People change. The kool-aid RELAXES me! That's *me*, relaxed!" She pointed at the monitor, where her video image blogged away. "It's THOSE IDIOTS," indicating the other, reasonable posts. "It's those bloggers, those 'REGULARS', who make me crazy! I'M DOING AN INTERVENTION ON THEM!"

"Since you're so reasonable and relaxed," said Rogue, "I'm sure you'll sit back down and listen." Mary Jo reluctantly sat, and sulked. "This is about free choice," Rogue continued. "Yours has been hijacked by the kool-aid. You went to that political rally as a blank slate. You were clueless, lacking a historical perspective. Easy prey for someone as slick as the Salesman. You've been politically corrupted, become a slave to someone elses agenda. You've stopped doing your own thinking because the one manipulating you gives you a warm fuzzy feeling and tells you to ignore facts and logic. Chad wants to give you back your free choice." She opened a cabinet with her thumbprint and two large bottles were revealed, one containing blue pills and the other containing red pills. She shook out one red pill and re-locked the cabinet.

"This," she told Mary Jo, holding up the red pill, "will wake you up. It'll take you out of the Beltway, let you see the real world."

"I like blue," Mary Jo insisted. "I like warm fuzzies. Why should I waste time with facts and thinking when people smarter than me can tell me what to think?"

"Big girls think for themselves," Rogue told her firmly. "How do you know that the people who tell you what to think are smarter than you, or even want what's best for you?"

"Because . . ." Mary Jo faltered.

"Because they told you so? And you trusted them?" asked Rogue. "Look, Mary Jo, I'll cut a deal with you. It's a win-win situation for you, no risk whatsoever. You saw the blue pills. How about you take this red pill, see what's really going on, then you can have the blue pill if you'd like to go back to the Beltway."

Mary Jo regarded her dubiously. "How can I . . ."

"Trust me?" Rogue laughed. "You don't have to trust me, you've got Chad! You trust him, don't you? Let's get him in here and see what he thinks about our plan." She pressed a button on the remote and spoke into it. "He'll be here in just a minute or two," she told Mary Jo, then looked closer at her. She opened a drawer and took out a brush. "How about we fix your hair a bit before he gets here?" she asked. "A face washing wouldn't hurt either." She moistened a washcloth and handed it to Mary Jo, who wiped off the kool-aid Joker's grin while Rogue brushed her hair.

Chapter 57
Coffee Break

"Hey, sport, wake up!" Ned shook Chad's shoulder.

"No-no-no," Chad moaned, then sat up suddenly. "It was you!" he told Ned. "You and Dog! You set a trap with that red carpet and when the Hollyweird celebs went onto the carpet, you opened fire and blew out the windows so I could escape!"

"Whoa, sport," Ned told him, "no one's shooting up anything. Must have been one heckuva nightmare!" He shook Chad's shoulder again. "Sure you're awake now? Your girlfriend's ready to see you, Rogue says go on in."

Chad stood up shakily. "It was so real," he told Ned, "so real." He started for the door leading to Mary Jo.

"Wait," said Ned, and handed him a huge enameled coffeepot. "Take this with you. Camp coffee. I made it myself, grew the coffee cherries, picked them, cured them, roasted them and ground them up. Brewed it over an open fire. Pour slow, the grounds are restless. Watch out for eggshells!"

Chad looked around the room and didn't see a fire or any means of making camp coffee. He shrugged, took the coffeepot and entered the room.

"Chad," said Rogue, sounding concerned, "you don't look rested at all." She took the coffeepot from him, sniffed appreciatively, took out mugs and began to pour.

"Nightmares," Chad muttered, and turned to Mary Jo. "Are you okay?"

"I'm alive," she snapped, "disappointed?"

"I'm sorry, Mary Jo," Chad began explaining in a rush. "Nothing like that was supposed to happen! I was so worried. I did everything I could to get you back, I thought I'd never see you again and it was all my fault!"

"Mary Jo," said Rogue, "Mikhail Smore was a wild card no one could have predicted. I really think it's in your best interests to wait until after you've taken the red pill to pass judgment on Chad's actions." She handed them mugs of the coffee.

"You'll take the red pill, Mary Jo?" Chad asked eagerly. "That's great! I couldn't go on living like we were, with your kool-aid addiction always coming between us. This is great! Our lives will be great! You'll see, Mary Jo, you won't regret this!"

Mary Jo looked at him coldly. "Why don't you put your money where your mouth is?" she asked him. "If I take the red pill, and don't like it, she," she nodded to Rogue, "said she'd give me the blue pill. So if I don't like the red pill world and decide I want the blue pill, if I'm so important to you, you'll take the blue pill too, won't you?" Her eyes narrowed and shot out electric blue darts. "If you want us to be together, and all, that is."

"Mary Jo," Chad began, looking intently at her, "I could tell you about all the things I've seen and all the things I've learned on this journey. I could tell you about the nightmare I just had, where the Republic was overthrown and our Flag was supplanted and a president turned himself into a king and sat on a throne. But I won't tell you all those things that made me believe that our country is being taken in the wrong direction. Instead I'll trust that once you take the red pill and break your kool-aid addiction, you'll see the facts and the reality of what's going on and how our country is at risk." Chad took a deep breath and held out his hand. "Mary Jo, you've got a deal."

"Oh, hell," said Mary Jo, and shook Chad's hand. She then turned her hand palm up and Rogue dropped the red pill into it. "Down the hatch," Mary Jo said glumly and tossed the red pill into her mouth. She washed it down with the coffee. "How long does this take tooo . . ." Her voice faded as she slumped and passed out.

"Quick!" said Rogue, "We have to act fast!" She pushed a button on the remote and the monitor came to life with hundreds . . . thousands . . . millions! . . . of faces of WE THE PEOPLE. She looked earnestly into the monitor and addressed the PEOPLE. "Men and women, girls and boys, citizens and patriots, a young woman is fighting a terrible kool-aid addiction and needs your help. She's taken the red pill, and if you believe, if you *really* believe, in our God-given rights, in the Constitution, in the Republic, in our nation's exceptionalism, in our American way of life, in our rugged individualism, in our desire to have people everywhere join us in freedom and prosperity, if you believe that America is not just good, but *great*, stand up and cheer! Cheer for the United States of America, cheer for life, liberty and the pursuit of happiness, cheer for freedom, cheer for this young woman and others like her to wake up and smell the coffee and join us in returning our country to what the Founders intended it to be!" And the PEOPLE jumped up and cheered!

"WE BELIEVE," they roared, *"WE BELIEVE!"*

Mary Jo stretched and inhaled deeply. Her eyelids fluttered. "Is that coffee I smell?" she murmured. Her eyes opened and she looked at Chad and smiled. "Chad! You made coffee! What a strange dream I've had, wait until you hear . . ." her voice faded as she took in her surroundings. She sat up. "I remember! It wasn't a dream!" She looked at Rogue, then back at Chad as WE THE PEOPLE faded from the monitor. "Oh no," Mary Jo moaned, head in her hands. "This is awful. I remember everything. I've been a horrible person. I can't believe it was me that did all those terrible things, that blogged so meanly to those nice people. Oh no," she continued, distraught, "what will I do?"

"You'll tell them you're sorry and you'll go on with a responsible life," Rogue said. "They'll understand that you were under the influence of the kool-aid and black ops hypnosis. Life goes on!"

"Mary Jo!" Chad exclaimed, elated. "You're free! This is great! How do you feel?" he asked her anxiously. "You don't want to take the blue pill, do you? You don't want *me* to take it, do you?"

"No, Chad," Mary Jo told him, "no blue pills, no kool-aid, ever again! My eyes are open and I like it that way. I'd rather make up my own mind than have anyone tell me what to think, say and do and how to act. Never again! I'm not a political virgin anymore!"

Deep in the woods, near the Alaska-Canada border, Mikhail Smore's clones stirred. They pulled their heads out of their asses with a loud 'pop' and looked around as Mikhail began to moan. He sat up an wiped red foam from his lips. "Why, that sneaky Slicky Willy!" he said, looking at the foam, "that wasn't the black pill! He slipped me the red pill!" The clones picked him up from the wreckage of the sleigh and dusted him off. "You know," he told the clones, "I think I'd like to make a movie! Maybe a documentary, something about corruption in government. I know!" he exclaimed, "WALNUT! I'll do an entire documentary on the corrupt ties between WALNUT and the politicians and the unions!" He linked arms with the clones and they began to walk south. "You'll see," he told them, "it'll be great, a huge hit!" He began to whistle 'The Star-Spangled Banner' as they walked.

Chapter 58
Vacation Plans

"Look, Mary Jo," Chad said, as they entered the mini-suite to clean up and wait until it was time to leave for home. "Our suitcases! I thought they were gone for good."

Mary Jo walked over to the luggage stand and opened her suitcase. She began to laugh, then pulled out items and tossed them into the air. Every single article of clothing was a shade of blue. "I guess I have some memory gaps," she told Chad. "I forgot that I dyed everything I own!"

"Yep," said Chad, "you just threw it all in the washer one day with a bunch of blue dye. You haven't worn any color but blue since."

"Hummm," said Mary Jo, fingering the clothing thoughtfully. "I want to say thank you, Chad, for everything you've done. If it wasn't for you, I'd have been stuck in that kool-aid addiction until it killed me. Really, you saved my life!"

"I had to try, Mary Jo, I couldn't leave you addicted if I could help you out of it."

"Thank you," Mary Jo said again. "But you know what, Chad? You never take me *anywhere*!" she stated emphatically.

"But, Mary Jo," Chad laughed weakly, "we've just been through the wilds of Canada and we're in Alaska now, about to travel back! How can you say that?"

"Well," she pouted, "we weren't exactly *together* on this trip, were we? Traveling *separately*, as I recall?" She glanced into a wall mirror, then stopped and peered closely at her reflection. "That kool-aid did a number on my complexion," she said, "my God, I'll have blue blackheads for six months!" She glanced at Chad, who stood nervously nearby. "*Vacation*, Chad, I need a *vacation!*"

"Our vacation's about to begin," Chad assured her, "we'll travel back through Canada and have a lot of fun, we can stay at that bed and breakfast place, rent bikes, go antiquing, whatever you want to do!"

"Been there, done that, got the tee-shirt." Mary Jo dismissed the idea. "I want a new and exciting vacation. Something completely different. I know we saw a lot of things on this trip, but do you know, Chad, what I've never, ever, *ever* seen in my entire life? Do you know what I want to see more than anything else in the world? A *Gulag*, Chad, I've never seen a *Gulag*! Can you imagine living for a whole twenty-seven years and never, ever seeing a *Gulag*? Oh, Chad," she exclaimed with false dismay, "I forgot! *You've* never seen a Gulag either, and you're older than me! So what should we do about this sad situation, Chad?" Mary Jo asked, sidling closer and toying with the buttons on his shirt.

"I, uh, uh . . ." stammered Chad, as Mary Jo used her fingernail to trace the ridges of his six-pack.

"Don't you worry about one itty bitty thing, Chad," Mary Jo cooed. "I know where there's a Gulag nearby – practically right on our way home. I bet they'd be glad to give us a tour. I already have the wardrobe for it!" Mary Jo laughed. "You could be my prisoner, Chad! Wouldn't that be fun?" Mary Jo's fingers tried to encircle Chad's wrists. She pushed his arms behind his back and plastered herself against his chest. "It'll be fun," she whispered, "trust me!"

"Okaaaaay," Chad gasped, "the Gulag . . ."

"Promise?" Mary Jo asked, darting her tongue between his shirt buttons and tracing tiny wet circles on his skin.

"P-p-p-promise," stammered Chad, breathing faster.

"Great!" Mary Jo exclaimed, releasing him and choosing her outfit from the scattered blue garments. "I'm taking a shower. Didn't they say we'd leave soon? They won't mind making this little detour, will they? You'll fix it, won't you, Chad?" She smiled brightly and blew him a kiss. "This is so exciting! I always wanted to be a spy. We'll find out why those Czars are building a Gulag, and who they want to put in it! The Illinois Combine – what a weird name for a Gulag!" She blew him another kiss and stepped into the bathroom. "And after that, we'll find something else exciting to do! I'll make them all pay for what they did to me, and I'll make sure they can't ever do it to anyone again!"

Chad sat on the edge of the bed and dropped his head into his hands. "The Gulag," he choked. "I promised to take her to the Gulag! What am I going to do now?"

"OW!" yelled Mary Jo from the bathroom.

"Are you okay?" Chad called out, as he jumped up. "What's wrong?"

"Duct tape," Mary Jo laughed. "There was duct tape on my butt! It hurt when I pulled it off. Care to help me rub baby oil on the sticky stuff it left on my butt?" she asked.

There was a knock at the door.

"Can't," Chad called out to Mary Jo as he went to answer the door. "company," he told her, "better hustle."

"Be out in a jiffy," she promised, and Chad heard the water begin to run.

Chapter 59
Trash Into Treasure

Chad opened the door and three men entered. Ned and Xo greeted Chad warmly and introduced him to the third member of their party, Stevahn. Ned was wearing his usual buckskins and was draped with weaponry of all sorts. The other two wore flight suits.

"Well, sport," Ned grinned and clapped Chad on the back, "all's well that ends well. Pretty soon you and Mary Jo will be riding, excuse me, *flying*, off into the sunset." He gestured to Xo and Stevahn. "Your trusty pilots will get you safely home."

"Uh," Chad began, "there's a bit of a problem. Mary Jo's not quite ready to go home. She wants a vacation, wants to do some sightseeing first. I don't think it's a good idea, but I kind of accidentally promised her. You'll tell her we can't do it, won't you? You'll tell her we have to go straight home?"

"Why, Chad Sixpack," Ned chided, "I'm surprised at you. Is the little lady cracking the whip? Can't tell her yourself?"

"I *promised*," Chad said, "it was an accident."

"What did she do, stick her tongue in your ear?" Ned asked. "Well? Don't leave me hanging, Chad!"

Chad looked embarrassed. "Something like that," he admitted.

The three men laughed. "Yeah, we've all been there," said Xo. "What's the problem with a little sightseeing? We could do that, no big deal. All the way to Niagara Falls, if you want!" He winked and punched Chad's arm.

"Keep it down," Chad begged, "she'll hear you. She doesn't want to go to Niagara Falls. She wants to go to . . ." he gulped, then whispered fiercely when the men leaned closer, ". . . *the Gulag!*"

"Whoa!" said Ned, taking a step back. "Actually . . ." he paused in deep thought for a moment, ". . . that's not a bad idea." Xo and Stevahn nodded in agreement.

"What?" asked Chad, also stepping back. "You can't be serious! I think she's slipped a widget, or something. She always wanted to be a spy, dresses up like Mata Hari or the Girl from U.N.C.L.E., or Emma Peel for Halloween every year – before her Blue Period, that is. What if she thinks she's really a spy?"

"Well?" asked Ned. "What if? What's the worst that could happen? She thinks she's a spy, she acts like a spy, she's got fancy spy training and crazy spy skills. I'm just not seeing a down side here, sport. Seems that would give her – and you – a better chance of infiltrating and surviving the Gulag."

"We could get you there," said Xo, "but you need a back story for cover, bona fides, weapons, extraction plan. The War Room could set it up in maybe a couple hours, just about how long it'll take us to get near the Gulag."

Just then Mary Jo came out of the bathroom, a vision in blue. "Hello," she greeted the men, and Chad introduced them to her. "So," she asked them, "are we going on a little adventure?"

"Mary Jo!" exclaimed Xo, taking her hand and tucking it into the crook of his elbow and steering her to the door. "Of course we are! Brilliant idea, simply brilliant! We just have to iron out a few logistics, they'll work on that while we're en route. Everything will be in place by the time we get there." He motioned to Chad, who picked up the bags and followed them. "Stevahn," Xo called, "you'll take care of . . .?"

"As usual," Stevahn grumbled.

Ned headed for the door too. "So long, guys, good luck! Stay in touch – we'll go hunting!" He turned in the other direction, on his way to the War Room to get the preparations started for the Gulag adventure.

Stevahn turned to look around the mini-suite and sighed heavily. He opened the desk drawer, then looked in all the cupboards and the dresser drawers. As he got on his hands and knees to look under the bed he began to mutter to himself.

"Let Stevahn do it. That's right, let him do the clean-up again. 'Police the room, Stevahn'," he mimicked. "'Leave no trace, no evidence.' Why me?" he groaned, as he got to his feet. "Why is it always *my* job?" He checked the closet and moved on to the bathroom.

"Hel-*lo*," he said, spotting a pair of bright blue fishnet stockings flung over the shower rod. He plucked them off the rod and tucked them into his flight suit pocket. He looked in the shower enclosure, in the cabinets and even in the toilet's water tank. He checked the trash can, and pulled out a wad of paper and duct tape. Noticing a fancy embossed seal, he carefully peeled the duct tape off. He set the documents on the sink counter with shaking hands. His eyes darted from document to document and he began to hyperventilate. He clutched his chest, reeling back against the wall.

"School records . . .," he whispered, "notarized foreign passport applications . . . born in Kenya . . .," his voice began to rise, "British subject . . . applications for foreign student scholarships and foreign student financial aid . . . Indonesian citizenship . . . Holy *CONSTITUTIONAL CRISIS*, Batman!"

Stevahn carefully folded the documents and put them in his jumpsuit. Taking a deep breath, he ran out of the room and headed after Ned at top speed.

THE END

About the Author

Dr. Kelly Swifte's entire career has been spent on sabbatical. This manuscript, The Saga of Mary Jo, is Dr. Swifte's first published work, and was brought to us by carrier pigeons. There may or may not be portions missing, as Dr. Swifte neglected to number the chapters, or the pigeons. Alas, the mystery deepens. Upon slaughtering the pigeons for examination by a forensic pathologist in order to gain clues about Dr. Swifte's whereabouts, it was discovered that the pigeons, each and every one, had been fed *an entirely different exotic diet*! Where and how did Dr. Swifte acquire these pigeons? Were they held captive by Dr. Swifte, and fed diets meant to deceive? Or did they indeed hail from all corners of the globe? Does Dr. Swifte have a pigeon in every port, flying chapters of the manuscript about willy-nilly, hot off the pen? But wait – if that were the case, *how did all the pigeons arrive at the abode of this humble agent at the exact same hour, nay, the exact same minute*?! Could Dr. Swifte have developed a delayed pigeon system? Were the pigeons collected during Dr. Swifte's extensive travels, then released at the chosen time and place? Most unfortunate, but upon further examination of the pigeon carcasses, some sort of demolition switch must have been activated. Not to worry, this agent shall not fail in the relentless pursuit of knowledge of Dr. Swifte's current location and situation. At this very moment, six Voodoo queens, Board-certified and veterans of the Jerry Springer show, are reading the pigeon entrails. I expect their report shortly, but the entrails are flung far and wide over tables, chairs, walls, the ceiling and the floor, so it's not an easy task. Rest assured, I will keep Dr. Swifte's faithful readers informed, whether of news in the entrails or the arrival of another flock of carrier pigeons bearing another manuscript. Until then, Ambrose B. Reston.